WILDCAT

A TEXAS ROMANCE

PHYLLIS KERR

CONTENTS

ACKNOWLEDGMENTS

Thank you to Carrie Peters
@cheekycovers.com
Cover and Website Design

To Brittany Mitchell Kerr
To Ashley Lord Kerr

Two Beautiful
And
Accomplished
Daughters-in-Law

PROLOGUE

*H*e crouched behind the far stall divider, unblinking stare locked on the side door, waiting for the slightest movement. He had to be quick. His eyes had adjusted to the thick darkness in about four or five minutes.

So would his.

Surprise, stealth, speed, he ticked off the plan in his mind. Precision and execution, he added. The door creaked and opened slowly. There he was highlighted from behind by the dimly burning lanterns hung along the board walk for late night patrons going home from the adult entertainment establishments offered by the town of Granbury, Texas.

"You in here? It's too dark to see."

"Got your note." He held up the note.

No answer.

"What do you want?" he called. No answer.

He heard a shuffling sound like boots moving softly on the dirt floor.

"Who's in here?"

Still, no answer.

He walked toward the sound, then stopped. In one swift movement, a strong arm wrapped around his head. Stinging, then wet sensations slid across his neck. He tried to turn around to confront his attacker, but his legs buckled at the knees and he collapsed to the ground. He tried to talk but all he heard was a gurgling sound. He felt a presence but couldn't't see who it was. He laid helpless, struggling to breathe, his lungs filling quickly with the wetness gushing from his neck. His eyes widened in panic. What is happening? he thought. Then all thoughts and movements ceased as the silencing darkness consumed him.

A STEADY HAND reached out and retrieved the note from his fingers then stuffed it in the dead man's breast pocket. The side door creaked a slow, sad song and a shadow slipped out and away.

PREFACE

GRANBURY TEXAS
1872

CHAPTER 1

*S*ugar Wylie pointed up at the gray-blue sky and yelled to her father, "Big storm rolling in." One of those nasty late winter, early spring noisy, blustery kind of storms that tries to scare a body into hiding under the bed, she thought, which is probably where her husband was after staying out all night.

She and her father, Quint Wylie, had ridden up to the north corner of their 1,800 square acre ranch, the Double Bar W, earlier that morning to look for any cattle that had strayed during the night.

"We better get going," Sugar said waving her coiled rope at the steers she had shooed into a group to drive back to the herd where the ranch hands waited, where her husband was supposed to be but wasn't, she added. "You go ahead," her father called over the growing sound of pre rain wind whipping up leaves and dirt all around them. "I hear a calf back here in the brush. I'll get him and catch up."

A sudden movement caught Sugar's attention in time

to see a young Comanche warrior wearing a buffalo raiding bonnet jump up from the brush, drop the calf he had been holding and draw back a sharp ended wooden lance ready to launch toward her father.

"Daddy! Look out!" she screamed as she pulled her Colt .36 six shot from its holster and fired a round inches over the startled brave's head. His lance hit the ground with a loud crack. Before Sugar had a chance to ready another shot, he took off running toward the Brazos river only feet away and dove in. Her father followed, but the boy had already disappeared into the roiling currant.

"Good shot, Baby Girl!" her father shouted.

"Thanks," she said her hand shaking from the adrenalin rushing through her body. She slid the six-shooter back into its place on her hip. "I'm glad he didn't't move, I almost hit him." She sounded relieved.

"Naw," he joked. "I taught you too good. He'll think twice about coming back here," Quint said acting like he faced attacks on his life every day.

"You did real good," he reassured her. "Let me catch this calf and get this lance and I'll be right with you."

"Ok," she said turning her attention back to her strays. A drop of rain splattered onto the top of her hat. She jumped then her hands started to shake again. Ever since childhood, just the sound of thunder in the distance had made her nervous. She would start to shake then run into her room and climb under the covers until the storm blew over.

She whistled to start her group of wandering troublemakers on their way. They moved slowly, reluctant to leave the patch of sweet new grass they had found. Circling around behind, she broke off a switch from a windblown Tallow and tried prodding them in the shanks to get them moving faster, but they paid her no mind and kept slowly ambling along.

I give up, Sugar thought, flipping the stick up in the air and watching it hit the ground. Rain or shine, cows didn't do anything unless they wanted to.

She tried to relax by leaning back into her saddle. She enjoyed the smell of wet leather and dampened plants, the sound of the rhythmic raindrops plopping in the dirt around her. The sway of the easy pace as they moved along usually left her feeling calm and relaxed, but not today, not until she arrived back where the rest of the herd waited, and she could hurry home.

"Hey, Cody," she called to one of the foremen who worked on the ranch as she rode up. "Nice weather."

Cody laughed and waved.

With her long silky black hair dripping down her back and her well-worn Levi's and button front blouse already soaked, she looked like her clothes were painted on. Most girls her age would want to die from embarrassment at this point, but Sugar didn't even notice. She saw no reason for embarrassment. She was with her family, her ranch hands. She had grown up thinking of them as brothers, working together for the same goal, keeping the ranch and its enterprises running smoothly to the benefit of them all.

Secretly, all the men in Granbury enjoyed looking at Sugar's ample curves, beautiful light blue eyes and infectious smile. She was a stunner. When she entered a room with her shiny black hair swinging in time with her tight rounded bottom, every head turned.

That's why her father had made a priority of teaching

her never show herself at disadvantage in front of her men. She would be the sole owner of the Double Bar W and The First Granbury Bank in town someday. She couldn't't lead men from a subordinate position. She had to be able to stand toe to toe with them, eye to eye, and not flinch when they tried to intimidate her.

Anyone who knew Sugar knew she needed no lessons in intimidation. Her father had been the perfect model for that. Quint Wylie, a bull of a man, standing over six feet tall with a wide barrel chest, represented the definition of intimidation every day of his life. No one pushed Quint Wylie around and anyone who tried better get ready to fight. He had instilled the same attitude in Sugar. The day she came home from school with her first black eye, he was so proud.

Carry on in his name. Uphold his honor in his absence. After eighteen years of unyielding instruction, Sugar had no problem doing just that. She could wrangle cattle, break horses, hunt small game, live out on the range, fight and shoot better than any average man. She didn't have to feel inferior to anyone. Not even her so-called husband.

Married off at the age of 14, Sugar still didn't understand why her father decided to make such a personal, life changing decision behind her back. She had begged for him to reconsider at the time, threatened to run away and even kill herself if forced to marry that stupid twenty-four-year-old Jordan. Marriage to the son of Arthur and Constance Averill, owners of the neighboring Rocking A Ranch that connected on the south with the Double Bar W, would join the two properties making the Wylie's and the Averill's the biggest landowners in Hood County. A match for the ages, her father told her. Both parents had signed legal agreements guaranteeing that Sugar and Jordan would marry and be equal partners to carry on the family legacy.

Quint looked so pleased with himself when he told Sugar the news that awful day the parents had signed the promissory contracts, but even though she stood to become a rich heiress, Sugar refused to see the good side of the arrangement.

Quint looked surprised when she ran out of the house and rode away to the only private place she had to go, the only refuge she had where she could get away from her father's ever-present voice in her head overriding any thoughts of her own. She had found an inlet off the Brazos River that ran alongside the western border of the Double Bar W. The Comanches called it Sleeping Lady Cove. Whenever Sugar wanted to hide, she ran to the cove.

Sugar loved her father. She wanted to please him, but sometimes he over-whelmed her until she felt she couldn't't breathe. A choking wave of anger would come over her cramping every muscle she had and shaking her body until she didn't't have enough strength left to shake anymore. She hated feeling weak after the episodes, Quint never allowed her to show weakness, so she didn't. She hid where no one could find her, kept her weakness to herself. In the long run, that made her feel stronger. Strong enough to do whatever her father told her to do because she was her daddy's perfect daughter. The daughter who had all the skills of a son, but none of a girl child. She was going to carry on Quint Wylie's name after he was gone, and he could live on in perpetuity through her. He built the kingdom, so she would carry the legacy. But what about the other half of her life? The half where she lived with the man she had selected to love? Not the man her father picked for her because he wanted his family's ranch.

Sugar needed to talk to someone about this but had no one else to turn to except her father. Her mother had abandoned them one night when Sugar was four years old. According to Quint, she had run away back to New Orleans with a gambling man leaving Sugar with him. He said her mother wanted to be a fancy woman and she didn't want Sugar around to ruin everything. But Quint had been a loving father. He had given her anything she wanted. She trusted him to protect her.

Now what? She thought. Was he going to leave her, too? What would become of her if he left her with this man she didn't know, expecting her to know how to be a wife?

In spite of persistent anxiety, she continued to try and accept her fate, even if her mind shouted, No! Finally, on her wedding day, she tried one more time to explain how much she did not want to marry Jordan Averill or anyone else right now. She was too young.

Quint patted her hand and gathered her into a gentle embrace.

"Hasn't Daddy always taken care of you, Sugar? You know I would never let that happen to my little girl."

"Yes, Daddy," she said forcing a tense smile, trying hard to believe him.

Quint lived up to his promise to her. He made it plain to Arthur and Constance Averill, Jordan's parents, that Sugar, far too young to leave home, would stay with him until her sixteenth birthday. Then Jordan could come and live at the Double Bar W and start learning about the ranch from him. At first, the Averill's refused to agree to Quint's plan.

"We were aware the children would be upset to find out they were obligated to an arranged marriage," Jordan's father had said. "But in a couple of years, when Sugar matures, she will grow used to being married. Jordan's a sweet boy. We're sure as they grow up together, build a family, everything will be fine," Jordan's father said. "They will come to understand that we have done the best thing for their futures."

Constance smiled and nodded her head.

Quint smiled but his bushy black eyebrows drew together to the middle of his forehead and his brown eyes narrowed. He looked at Constance then Arthur.

"Sugar and I have decided ours is the right course to take."

Disappointed, the Averill's actually had other plans for Sugar. They thought they would have her under their control to mold her into a compliant wife, maybe see that Jordan gave her two or three babies right away to keep her busy. Then when Quint passed on, sooner rather than later they hoped, Jordan could take over the ranch and bank and Sugar could stay home and raise the children. Now they had to wait two years to enact their plan and neither of them were getting any younger.

"It's going to be a long two years," they all thought.

To Sugar's mind, though, two years seemed a long way away. And Daddy had brought home that beautiful Arabian stallion for her as a wedding present. Married life was a long way away and like Daddy said, a lot could happen in two years. But two years turned out to be not such a long time and on her sixteenth birthday Jordan showed up, possessions in hand, ready to do his husbandly duty.

None of the parents realized how much their children didn't want to be married until Sugar and Jordan had to live together in the same house. Quint didn't't help matters, either. As soon as Jordan moved in, Quint sat him down in his study and explained in minute detail what he expected from his son-in-law.

Jordan protested immediately.

"You want to make a ranch hand out of me?" Jordan said in a tight voice.

"What did you think you were going to be?" Quint sat forward in his chair.

Jordan leaned back.

"I don't know anything about ranching. I never had anything to do with it at home."

Quint blew out a breath like an old bull.

"I thought I would run the bank?" Jordan said

"The bank? I didn't't think about the bank. I guess we can start you training as a teller. Then in five years or so..."

"No!" Jordan looked up at Quint. "I'm your son-in-law. I should at least start as a Vice President."

Quint smiled at him.

Jordan jumped up.

Quint stood and looked Jordan straight in the eye keeping his voice slow but emphatic.

"I see. Well, I don't need a Vice President." His voice strained with the effort to speak softly. "I need a ranch hand. If you are available for that, I have a place for you. If not, I'm going to have to rethink this whole business."

They stared at each other until Jordan realized Quint was not going to blink.

"I'll give it a shot." He said and walked out of the house.

Two years later, Sugar and Jordan cared even less about each other than before.

During their time apart, Jordan found plenty of companionship away from home and Sugar felt happy with that. They only spoke to snipe at one another. His parents found solace in strong drink and shopping in the growing party town of Fort Worth. Quint became active in civic issues in Granbury. They all lived happily apart, for a while.

CHAPTER 2

*J*ordan finally moved into his room at the Double Bar W. Sugar had spent the last two years growing into a beautiful young woman. Quint had been worried that Jordan, in a rush to get his hands on his new bride, would insist on an adjoining bedroom to Sugar's but when Jordan followed tall, muscular twenty-four-year-old Cody Edwards to the bedroom upstairs and on the other side of the house from Sugar, Jordan seemed pleased with the accommodations.

The room, much larger than his at home, had a nice sized bed for sleeping, a narrow day bed for napping, two armoires for clothes and boots, a bureau for smaller items and a water closet for his exclusive use. He could bathe and shave in the ranch hand's bath house outside.

"This is really fine," Jordan told Cody, "better than the room I had at home," he said, laughing. He walked over to the bed and tested the springs. "No squeaks." He grinned at Cody.

Cody looked down at the floor.

"You know all the hands around here, especially me, think of Sugar as a baby sister."

Jordan nodded, "Yea?"

Cody looked at Jordan.

"We won't take kindly to any loose talk about anything she says or does. Do you get what I mean?"

Jordan clenched his teeth. He felt an angry heat creeping up his face.

"What kind of jerk do you think I am?" Jordan asked.

Cody smiled.

"Just giving some advice."

He walked to the open door.

"If you need anything, let me know."

Cody nodded his head once and ducked under the door jam.

Big deal. Big man, Jordan thought.

"You know you're talking to your new boss, don't you?" he said to the empty space Cody had just exited. Jordan picked up one of his satchels and slammed it on the bed.

SUGAR WATCHED out the window at Cody and Jordan walking into the house. Her first plan of the day had been to go away somewhere, anywhere so as not to have to face that man Daddy made her marry, she thought. But as Daddy would say, "Better to stand face to face with your problem right off than to keep seeing it every day until you do."

But Daddy hadn't been married off to some stranger he

didn't like the looks of and didn't't know anything about what was expected of him in the bedroom.

She opened her vanity drawer and took out what looked like an old rag. She held it lovingly to her cheek as if she were handling an ancient relic of great value.

Daddy was right, of course, she thought, looking in the mirror of her vanity wishing the person in the mirror knew at least some of the answers to the questions that kept going around in her mind. She wanted to just be friends for a while before she had to give herself to him, but how could she tell him that. She had never even talked to him. She couldn't't imagine herself going to his room and taking her clothes off for him to look at her. It sounded so degrading. No. She couldn't't do it, she thought. What am I going to do? she asked the girl in the mirror.

You are going have to think of something, the girl in the mirror answered back.

She wrapped the rag around her wrist like a bracelet.

Let's see, she thought moving over to the bed to sit. How do I start? I need to talk to a woman. If I had a mother, she could help me.

She looked down at the rag on her wrist. A mother would know how to handle this. But if I had a mother, she reasoned, I probably wouldn't be in this fix to begin with. Sugar removed the rag bracelet, stretched it out and spread it carefully across her pillow. Laying down on the pillow, she could clearly see in her mind the inside of the closet where she had found it so many years ago.

She had been six years old and loved to explore her giant house. All sorts of treasures waited in old cupboards and corners for her to discover and raid. She waited impatiently every day for Daddy to come home to show him what she had found and where she had found it. They enjoyed this time together until the day she found the secret room in the attic.

The door had been hard to open. She looked for a long time for a key to open it. When she finally found one, the door opened to a young girl's fantasy land. She saw lots of pretty things inside. She remembered the shoes and old dresses and sparkly things that looked like glass she could clip in her hair and wear around her neck. But the one thing that caught her eye was the dress, the beautiful white dress with sprinkles of glass and delicate webbed material draped over the shoulders sparkling in the sunlight from the window. She managed to pull the pretty material down off the hanger and take it to her room to hide and later show Daddy what she had found. But Daddy hadn't been happy to see the interesting room she had found. He took the pretty cloth away from her and told her to never go in that room again. She cried. But later she sneaked back and cut a piece of the pretty dress and hid it in her room so Daddy couldn't't find it and take it away again. Later he apologized for fussing at her and explained the best he could that the dress had belonged to her mother and seeing the dress made Daddy feel bad.

"Don't go in that room ever again," he told her.

She found out later from the housekeeper that the beautiful dress was her mother's wedding dress.

She understood not to go in the room. She didn't't want to make Daddy feel bad again. But understanding why it made Daddy feel bad took years. She kept the swatch of lace. The fact that no one knew made it feel more special. Sometimes, like today, she took it from the drawer to hold. An immediate feeling of comfort enveloped her, a sense that everything would be all right, or at least a six-year-old's version of alright.

SHAKING OFF THE MEMORY, Sugar rolled over on her back and looked at the ceiling. One thing she knew in her favor, Jordan had other women, Sugar reasoned returning to the task at hand. What would he want with her? It's money he and his parents were after. Maybe she could have a lawyer make them an offer to buy back the contract.

She sat up and looked at her pillow covered in the old lace.

Or maybe she could make Jordan an offer? She knew he could be bought.

Sugar felt better once she had some options. She decided to get to work and let the ideas marinate for a while.

Dressed in her old Levi's and faded chambray work shirt, boots and well-worn Stetson, she headed out to start her day. She always started in the stable. That way she could groom and saddle Magic, her Arabian stallion, and take him out for her morning rounds checking on the in-process work projects of the ranch. Each man was assigned specific projects to ramrod. If the projects were not finished by assigned project date, they had to report to Quint and explain why.

Now that Quint accepted the Chairmanship of the Railway Committee in Granbury, and the board position of the Fort Worth Committee, his schedule called him away from the ranch more than he wanted but the

Railway Project meant a huge boost to the economic condition of Granbury as well as making the movement of herds of cattle easier and more profitable. The entire community of Hood County stood on the brink of the largest boom the area had ever seen, if the railroad came through.

In order for Quint to accomplish these goals, he put Sugar in charge of some of his tasks on the ranch. Considering she had been one of the hands mending fences, babysitting cattle, and sometimes berthing calves, she thought riding around on Magic and watching others work was a pretty good job. She checked on the progress of all the work projects for each day, consulted with Cody then returned to Quint's home office and documented the progress in the daily journal.

Sugar relished the sense of accomplishment at the end of that day as she sat outside watching to catch Jordan before he got away for the evening. The idea of having to wait another day to have their talk made her feel light-headed, on the verge of panic. She needed to get these issues settled before she lost control and did something desperate that Daddy wouldn't't like.

The men looked tired and ready to wash up for supper. But first the horses needed a bath and brushing before feeding and bedding down for the night. She watched each man keeping a mental tally of who took this task seriously and who didn't't when she realized Jordan hadn't come in.

She stood and walked around to look for him.

If he is here, I don't see him, she thought. Cody walked by leading his horse to the water trough for a much-needed drink.

"Hey, Cody," she called to him. "How did your day go?"

"Okay," he said removing his hat.

"Had a little trouble around lunch time."

He sounded reluctant to talk.

"Something I can help you with?" Sugar said.

"Maybe," he said looking down at his hat. "Jordan left around lunch time."

"Left? Why?"

"Said he was feeling sick. Said he wasn't used to working out in the sun."

Sugar stared at him for a minute.

Cody continued.

"I told him he could go sit under a tree and get some water. Take a break. It would pass. He didn't't like that. Said he was leaving and if I said anything about it to you or Quint, he would fire me."

Sugar's eyebrows lifted and her eyes opened wide.

"What?" she said. "He said that?"

"Yup," he said looking a little peeved himself.

Sugar placed her hand on his arm.

"I'm so sorry, Cody. Please don't pay any attention to what he says. I'll speak to him right now. You're impor-tant to me. I need you here. Daddy put me in charge of task monitoring. I really need your help."

She felt his arm relax. His gaze lifted to look into her pale blue eyes.

"I'm not going anywhere, ma'am. You can count on me."

Sugar realized she had been squeezing his arm. She let go.

"Thank you." She smiled at him, turned and walked toward the house.

He watched her walk away.

"Rachel," Sugar called to Rachel Strom, the house-keeper, as she walked in the front door.

"Yes, Sugar. I'm in the parlor," she called back.

Sugar walked to the parlor to find her dusting the furniture.

"Hi," she said giving the middle-aged woman a hug.

Shorter and thinner than Sugar, she looked like a schoolteacher or dance instructor, but she worked harder than just about anybody on the ranch. She kept the large ranch house clean, cooked for Quint and Sugar and many of the ranch hands. She made the home run smoothly. And she had been taking care of Sugar since she was a baby.

"Have you seen Jordan today?" Sugar asked her.

"No, I haven't," she said continuing to dust the marble topped side table. "I thought he went out to work."

I did too, Sugar thought.

"Okay, thanks," she said and went to her room to wait. Two hours later Rachel called her to dinner. Sugar knew Quint had traveled to Fort Worth for a Railway Committee meeting and would not return until tomorrow afternoon. She dined alone and took a book on crop irrigation to the parlor to read and listen for Jordan to come home. The next sound she heard was Rachel fussing at her.

"Sugar, you all right? Have you been here all night?"

"What?" Sugar said looking around in confusion. Then she remembered. "Is it morning?" she asked.

"Yes, Darlin' ," she said.

"Did Jordan come in yet?"

"Not that I know of," she said.

Just then, the door opened, and they heard Jordan's voice murmuring unintelligibly.

"Jordan, where have you been all night?" Sugar called.

He walked into the parlor. Sugar could tell he had been drinking. He spied a bottle of Quint's bourbon and some glasses sitting on a tray on top of a large buffet. He walked over and filled a glass taking a long drink then looked at her.

"Don't talk to me in that tone and it's none of your concern where I've been."

Rachel's mouth dropped open and she stepped in front of Sugar.

"Do not talk to Sugar like that!" she shouted at him.

Jordan looked at her through blurry red eyes.

"Shut up! I'm going to bed."

He went up to his room.

Sugar hesitated then hurried after him.

"Don't go up there!" Rachel tried to stop her.

"He's not getting away with this," Sugar said. Rachel could already see Sugar's cheeks turning red.

That's not good Rachel thought.

Upstairs, Jordan was trying to lock the door, but Sugar kicked it open before he could turn the lock.

"Just a minute," she said. "You leave work without checking in, stay out all night, come home drunk, and abuse Rachel? Just who do you think you are?"

He looked her up and down then blew out a loud laugh spitting expensive bourbon on Sugar and all nearby furniture.

"I am your husband, My Dear. That's who I am. So, either take off those clothes and lay in that bed or get the hell out of my room," he yelled starting toward her.

In one swift movement, Sugar swung her booted foot upward landing a solid kick on Jordan's shin.

Jordan let go a loud yelp and fell to the floor grabbing the painful leg with both hands.

Sugar waited to see if he was going to get up, but he seemed too lost in misery to try.

"You are no husband of mine," she yelled down at him. "Pack your stuff and get out of my house!"

Just then Cody came running in with Rachel right behind. He looked at Sugar, then at Jordan and started laughing.

"He's drunk." Sugar growled and walked out of the room.

Cody, still laughing, grabbed Jordan's arm and pulled him to his knees.

"Some more advice," Cody bent down and whispered in Jordan's ear, "That's why we call her Wildcat."

Cody helped Jordan stand. "Come on," he said, "I'll take you to the bunkhouse. You'll be safer there and you can sleep off the liquor, so you'll be in better shape for when her daddy comes home this afternoon. You think she kicks hard!"

Cody shook his head and laughed all the way to the bunkhouse.

CHAPTER 3

*J*ordan forced his rummy blue eyes open enough to find out where he had landed after his all-night bender.

Looks like a bunk house, he thought, opening his eyes slightly wider, careful not to go too far and let the bright sunlight in to cause one of those ice pick headaches that mixing rot gut whisky and expensive bourbon in large amounts always caused.

He scanned the walls hoping to find some clue as to which bunkhouse he had stumbled into. A red sign over the door read Double Bar W.

Oh, no he thought shaking his head. Anywhere but here. His mouth opened wide and he sucked in a full breath of air in a mind clearing yawn. He thought back to the previous night trying to remember what had happened after he left work.

Keeping one hand on the cot, he slowly stood. He still had his boots on, he realized. He started toward the door but stopped. His left boot top rubbed against a sore spot that hadn't been there before. He bent over and pulled up his trouser leg. A large black bruise, about the size of a two-dollar pancake, wrapped halfway around his calf and shin. The shades of black varied starting lighter around the edges then darkening at the two-bit sized black lump swollen in the center.

"What the-," he started to swear then the image of Sugar with her boot moving in slow motion played in his mind. His leg hurt all over again.

"That Bitch," he said gently rubbing his leg.

Several visions of revenge ran across his mind somewhat soothing his anger until reality set in spoiling his fun. Quint would be home soon, and his pushy father-in-law surely would want to talk to him. He hurried outside to see if Quint had returned yet. He didn't't see anyone around. Someone had tied his horse just outside the bunkhouse. He needed to leave, now, he thought. He hurried out to his horse, tightened his cinches, mounted and headed out in the direction of the Rocking V.

At home, Jordan led his horse into the stable and hung a bag of oats around his neck. He hoped his mother hadn't seen him ride up.

"Jordan is that you," his mother's voice called from outside.

"In here," he said.

Constance Averill walked through the stable door, a concerned look on her face.

"What's wrong?" she asked.

"Sugar got mad and attacked me." He pulled up his pant leg.

"Oh, my stars! What happened?

"You know Sugar," he said. "She has a temper. I had to

go to town yesterday to have my cinch fixed. It's still not right." He raised the stirrup on his saddle and showed her the cinch. "See how loose it is?" He shook the cinch and it rattled. "I've been needing to get it fixed, but we've been so busy at the ranch I haven't been able to get over to Bailey's to get parts."

"We weren't really busy yesterday, so I went on and when I got back, she jumped me for not telling her I was leaving. What do I have to do, report to her every time I have to go somewhere? Am I a prisoner or something?" He looked hurt.

His mother hugged him.

"Of course not!" she said. "You don't have to answer to her. She's just your wife."

"That's what I told her." He gave her his little boy look.

"What's wrong with that girl?" his mother said and straightened his hair with her hand. "You don't even have your hat. It's hot out here."

"I know Mamma. She can be mean. I hate the thought of going back there."

"You don't have to go back right now. Come on in. You need to tell your father about this."

"Have some of Mamma's biscuits and chicken. That'll make you feel better." She led him out of the stable toward the house.

Inside, Arthur Averill sat at the kitchen table reading a week-old copy of the Ft. Worth Gazette. He looked up to see Constance helping Jordan to a chair.

"What happened, Son?" He folded the paper and set it down on the table.

"That crazy girl you married me off to, that's what happened."

Constance petted Jordan's shoulder to calm him down and shot a stern look at her husband.

"Jordan's had a hard night," she answered for him.

"I see. Tell me about it," he said looking from Constance to Jordan.

"Show him your leg," Constance said shaking her index finger at Jordan's leg.

Jordan lifted his pant leg to expose the swelling bruise.

"My Lord!" Arthur swore. "Did a mule kick you?"

"Yes," Jordan said, "a mule named Sugar."

His father looked at him then Constance.

"What did you do to her?" he asked as if he really didn't't want to know the answer.

"Nothing! I left work early to get some repair parts for my saddle cinch and when I got back, she was waiting for me. I no more than walked in the door and she jumped me and told me to get out of her house. So, I left. I'm not going back."

Arthur exhaled slowly and looked at Constance. He stared at his hands for a minute then at Jordan.

"Son, you know you have to go back. This is too important to throw away over a silly argument."

"This is no silly argument! Look what she did to me!"

"Is it worth throwing away a fortune over? Is it worth trading a life of prosperity and ease for that of a common rancher? Stop and think! Get your temper under control."

"Am I supposed to turn into a whipped dog, afraid of every move she makes?"

"No, of course not. But how hard would it be to put your head down and do your work? Stay out of her way. Go on about your business and don't talk to her. If she talks to you, keep it short. No emotion. Too much is at stake here. Just hang in there. You never know what the future might bring."

Jordan stared at his father. What was he saying? Jordan thought. That something bad could happen to Sugar leaving him the sole owner of both ranches and the bank, too.

Jordan sat back in his chair and studied his father's smiling face. Maybe he's not so dumb after all, he thought, as a new idea sprung to life in his head.

"You are right, Dad," Jordan said letting the roots of the new idea germinate in his creative imagination. "I can do that."

He hugged his mother and shook his father's hand.

"Get this boy a cold compress for his leg, Constance," his father said and passed him a plate of fried chicken.

QUINT WALKED into the parlor at the Double Bar W to find Sugar waiting to talk to him. The trip to Ft. Worth had been pleasant. So pleasant that Quint felt as if he had attended a four-day nonstop party and all he wanted to do for the rest of the day was sleep and eat home cooking then sleep some more.

Sugar knew she should let him alone for the rest of the day, but as soon as she heard his voice her anger and frustration broke free and her story of how Jordan had acted spilled over her better judgement and tumbled out of her in bits and pieces between deep gulps and injured tears.

Quint, still holding his travel pelisse, stared at her for a minute, set the pelisse on the floor, and grasped her with both hands. He held her at arm's length turning her from side to side to check for any physical injuries, then looked deep into her eyes to see if some sort of hysteria had over-taken her. Seeing neither injuries nor madness, he set her on the sofa and sat beside her.

"Calm down. You know I can't understand you when you are over wrought. Rachel, bring a glass of cool water to the parlor please," he called.

Rachel hurried in with a mug of water and handed it to Quint. She gave Sugar a worried glance then returned to the kitchen.

"Here," he said and placed her shaking hands around the mug. She took it and drank the water down in one gulp. Quint hugged her until he felt her muscles relax.

"Now," he said gently, "tell me what happened."

Sugar sat up straight and gathered all the composure she could and told her story again in a calmer manner. She told Quint about Jordan leaving work early without telling anyone, how he had stayed out all night and come in drunk, how he had spoken to her and Rachel and how she had to kick him to stop him from attacking her. In her trembling voice she told him once more how she did not want to be married to Jordan.

"Come, come," he patted her on the back as if she were one of the ranch hands. "You haven't even given this marriage a chance."

Sugar looked down at the floor and shook her head.

"All of this is new to both of you," he said. "You're both nervous. This is going to take time to get to know each other in order to make a rational judgement about your futures. Give it some time, Sweetheart. I'm sure the more you work with him the more you will find him falling in love with you and wanting to stay home and be a good husband."

Sugar could not believe what her father was saying. He hadn't understood a word she had said. He is just treating her like a child and telling her to do what Daddy says, she thought

Sugar lifted her head, straightened her shoulders and looked her father in the eyes to see if he truly was delusional. The problem is not working with Jordan, she thought. The problem is the idea that she would be sleeping with this man sharing her most private intimacies. She already knew in the depths of her womanhood that she would never willingly share herself with him. How could she build a happy life without feeling love?

Quint watched her with anticipation. Surely, she knew he only wanted the very best for her, he thought.

"All right, Daddy," she said in a half whisper. She knew fighting with him was useless. She stood, walked to her bedroom and turned down the lanterns.

CHAPTER 4

*S*ugar looked out her window and watched the pink horizon lighten to a glowing purple before dragging herself out of bed.

How was she going to get through this day? she kept asking herself as she baby stepped her way to the wash basin and splashed cold water on her swollen face. What is wrong with you? she said to the mirror after making her way to the vanity and plopping down on the white velvet covered stool.

My life, she answered herself.

Her neck ached as if she had been balancing a heavy weight across her shoulders. Her eyes stung as if she had been crying all night. She had never felt so defeated. She had wanted to tell her father that his advice to wait and hope for the best sounded like advice for a child who had lost her new puppy. Not a grown woman entering into a future that would make her miserable for the remainder of her life. Just saying the word hope left her feeling forsaken and alone.

If she had been a boy, she thought, Daddy wouldn't have had a problem. A son could have inherited the family empire and carried on without a hitch. A son wouldn't have had his life sold out from under him as she had like some kind of chattel having to be bartered for a male primogeniture to take her place.

I do know some bartered women, she thought. One in particular who her Daddy knew.

She had met Ginger North several times. Her father had escorted her to some community socials and get togethers at the ranch. He visited her once or twice a week at the Social Club where she managed the ladies who worked there, bartered women in their own way. Maybe they could answer some questions for her or even offer some advice to help her situation.

The idea sounded good. If she finished her chores early enough, she might ride over to the Social Club to see what they have to say.

Sugar stepped into her Levi's, buttoned up a nicer than usual blouse, pulled on work boots and hat and headed for the kitchen to find some breakfast.

The kitchen smelled like freshly made, hot coffee. Rachel must be around here somewhere, Sugar thought helping herself to a generous mugful to take with her.

Magic acted glad to see Sugar when she carried her coffee out to the stable. He danced around the stall playing catch me if you can, making saddling him a much more difficult project than usual. Once finally ready, Sugar climbed up on the shiny black stallion and the pair started out for the daily chores.

Sugar loved the crisp, quiet coolness of early Spring mornings. She loved to watch the glorious awakening sun flare like molten satin gold along the horizon, beautiful now, but hinting at the rising temperature in store for the afternoon to come. She especially loved to wander across the grassy plain and watch the Sleeping Lady Peak appear through the mist as she rode closer to her cove.

"Sugar!" a voice shouted from behind jarring her out of her reverie. She turned in her saddle to see Cody riding toward her on his reddish-brown gelding. She gently pulled on Magic's reins to bring him to a stop.

"What are you doing up so early?" he said catching up to her. "I saw you riding by and waved but you kept on going. I wanted to be sure you were okay."

She laughed and leaned over to pet Magic's gracefully arching neck.

"I didn't sleep well last night. I was probably falling asleep. Good thing you saw me. Although I'm pretty sure I would have come to when I reached the cove. It's so early, I thought that would be a nice place to sit and drink my coffee."

She held up her cup.

"Sounds good. Care if I come along?" he said

"Sure."

She kneed Magic into a slow walk and Cody followed.

"You know," Sugar looked at Cody's horse, "I don't know your horse's name."

Cody laughed. "Horses don't have names."

Sugar looked surprised.

"Yes, they do."

"What's your horse's name?" Cody's hazel eyes shone with amusement. The morning breeze ruffled his sandy blonde hair.

"I'm not going to tell you if you're going to laugh at me," she said in feigned affront.

Cody laughed. "I'm not laughing at you."

"Yes, you are. Just for that, if you really want to know his name, you are going to have to guess it," she said looking serious.

"No, no, no, I really don't care what his name is, unless it's Blackie?" He lifted his tawny eyebrows and slightly tilted his head.

"Is that a guess?" she retorted, lifting her eyebrows in kind.

"No. That's not a guess," he said looking around at what looked like an entrance to a small wooded area. He followed Sugar inside. The trees opened into a closed-in grassy embankment surrounding a clear lagoon of shimmering water.

"Is this the cove?" He looked around. "This is cozy," he said.

"I love it here," Sugar said. "It's quite and relaxing. The water is warm enough in the afternoon for a swim."

"I bet that's refreshing after a long hot day," Cody said sounding truly impressed.

"It is," Sugar said and dismounted Magic without spilling a drop of coffee. "Let me heat this up," she said.

Cody watched as Sugar gathered some rocks, two sticks, some dead brush and proceeded to create a small ember with the two sticks. She dropped the ember onto the stack of dry brush she had formed on the ground. The ember flamed instantly. She placed the rocks in a small circle on top of the flames then set the coffee mug on the rocks.

"It'll only take a minute or two," she said watching to be sure the flames stayed under control.

They watched the coffee heat for a few minutes. Sugar used some fallen leaves to insulate the handle so she could lift the hot cup and hold it out for Cody.

"Ladies first," he said stepping over to what looked like a soft place and sat down.

Sugar followed and sat beside him. She looked out at the water and took a sip of coffee.

"Perfect," she said handing the cup to Cody.

"Delicious," he agreed, then said, "You okay?"

"Why do you ask?" She took another sip of the warm coffee. She knew he meant the incidents involving Jordan, but she didn't't want to talk about them right now.

"No reason." He looked around at the opening where they came in. "I better get back to work." He stood up. "I have a mean boss and she's going to dock my pay if she catches me sitting around drinking coffee."

Sugar laughed.

"I have a boss too and whatever your boss does to you, he'll do twice to me."

They both laughed.

Cody swung up on his horse and said, "See you and Licorice later."

"That's not it," Sugar said shaking her head.

"I don't care, anyway, horses don't have names,"

Cody said, tipped his hat, and rode out of the opening.

"He's a nice guy," she thought watching him go.

She sat awhile listening to the day dawn then stood and slung the dregs left in the bottom of the cup onto the hot rocks that heated the coffee. The rocks hissed and steam rose while she made sure all fire had been extinguished.

Magic didn't't play with her like before in the stable. This time he was ready to follow Cody's horse out on the open plain to run off his early morning energy. He strutted through the opening then took off at a flat out run. Sugar sat up straight and guided him toward the next stop of the day. She loved to feel the power of his athletic body running effortlessly through the prairie grasses, feeling the cool morning air whip her hair wildly across her face. She waived at Cody as they blazed by wondering what name he would think of next for Magic.

The day passed much as usual. Sugar finished her chores a little after lunch time. She decided to ride home for a change of clothes then sat at her father's desk and recorded her day's progress into the daily log.

The bronze clock on the fireplace mantel chimed two o'clock. If she hurried, she could ride to the Social Club, talk to Ginger and get back by supper. She went to her room and took enough money from the cash in her small wall safe to buy a drink and have a little extra just in case.

Sugar rode what she called her work horse, Jonnie, up to the front of the Granbury Social Club. The white wooden building stood three stories high with four large ground to roof Grecian style pillars along the front of a wide portico. Groups of mostly men, but some women sat and stood around talking, drinking and enjoying the afternoon. Some of them turned and stared at Sugar walking up the steps, but she didn't't pay any attention. The door stood open and she walked in. A friendly looking young woman approached her.

"Hello. Aren't you Quint's kid, Sugar?" she said.

"Yes, I am. Do you know my Daddy?" Sugar said.

"Oh yes," she said, "everybody knows Quint! Nobody can miss that big voice of his," Maddie laughed. "But he's not here. He doesn't usually come in until later in the evening to see Ginger."

"Is she busy?"

"I don't know," she looked around at the crowd. "Sit here on this stool and I'll go find her."

"Thank you, I'm sorry, what is your name?"

"I'm Maddie Burrell," she said smiling.

"Thank you very much, Maddie."

"You're welcome" she said and went to find Ginger.

Sugar didn't't have to wait long. Ginger emerged from a backroom door carrying a box of full champagne bottles. She handed the box to one of the men who acted as security, bar keeper and porter and hurried over to Sugar.

"Sugar what's wrong? Is Quint all right?"

"Daddy's fine. There's no emergency. I needed someone to talk to and you seemed like the right person," she said.

Ginger took Sugar's hands in hers. "Of course, Baby, you can always come to me. Let's go up to my room where we can have some privacy."

She hugged Sugar and led her to the third floor where only the women were allowed to go. Guards patrolled these rooms day and night to guarantee the Social Club hostesses safe and secure spaces for her own private use. Anyone who tried to violate this space felt the full punishment of the House including physical retribution and immediate and permanent expulsion. This was an important rule for everyone, and everyone respected it.

Ginger seated Sugar in her most comfortable chair and drew another chair closer for herself.

Sugar took a slow look around the room paying particular attention to the bed. Was there anything special or different about this bed? What about the furniture or the arrangement of the furniture that could be considered special? She noticed the odor, a pleasant lavender fragrance wafting around her. A casually arranged vanity space with a delicate oak table carved all over with curling vines of tea roses winding around the legs and corners, and a large dressing screen to project the desire for modesty which actually converted to seduction when noted that the semi-transparent screen was constructed of a fine black lace that provided glimpses of a freed breast or the curve of a soft hip, made up most of the furnishings.

Sugar looked at Ginger with a new appreciation of her ingenuity. She had taken a few carefully selected furniture pieces and created an atmosphere precisely suited to her purposes.

"Would you like something to drink? A glass of wine or whisky?"

"Thank you," Sugar said turning her full attention back on Ginger. "A glass of whisky would be wonderful."

Ginger poured the whisky with graceful movements as if teasing the amber liquid into the glass. Sugar noted every aspect of Ginger's presentation of herself to try them out when she returned home, because, Sugar surmised in her present mood, a woman who possessed the power of seduction and knew how to wield it possessed the power of control over a man that she needed to survive right now.

Ginger held out the crystal glass for Sugar and she took it thanking her and emulating her same movements.

"You wanted to talk to me?" Ginger took a sip of whisky she had poured for herself.

"Yes. Thank you for seeing me. I know how busy you are. I am in an uncomfortable place in my life right now." Ginger nodded her head as if she understood exactly what has been happening in her life.

"I am trapped in a loveless marriage and I don't know what to do or how to handle the situation. I'm sure you know Jordan Averill?" Sugar took a sip of whisky.

"Very well," Ginger said.

"I think he has a girlfriend here. You probably see him more than I do."

"Probably," Ginger nodded her head then a concerned look came over her face.

"Don't worry. I don't want to break that up." Sugar assured her. "I want somehow to learn to live with it."

Sugar would have been willing to bet that Ginger didn't't shock easily, but she looked shocked right now.

"In fact, I want them to get together. The closer they grow, the more likely they will want a home and children. The more likely he will be to defy his parents and leave me."

She took another sip of whisky.

"I can go back to making my own life with a man I have selected. I want someone who loves me not my money. I'm not free to find this man right now with this so-called marriage I'm stuck in. Daddy is dead set for me to have Jordan and he has closed the discussion and won't talk to me about it anymore. You know Daddy."

"Indeed, I do."

They both laughed. Sugar let out a sigh and went on.

"I knew another woman would understand my problem. It's hard when you don't have a mother," her voice broke at the end of her sentence. She cleared her throat and sipped her whisky.

Ginger leaned forward and squeezed Sugars hands.

"I'm so glad you came to me. I don't know what I can do about this, but I can tell you some things that will help you."

"I would appreciate that," Sugar said feeling some better just having someone listen to how she felt.

"I knew your mother before you were born."

Sugar stared at the floor for a moment.

"Really?" she said.

"It was many years ago. I don't remember exactly how many. We were very young. It was even before your father knew her. You are so like her. You could have been twins except for your eyes. You have the same build, the same hair, the same voice. The only difference is your eyes. Your mother had very dark eyes, black I would say, which seems odd with you having such light eyes."

Sugar felt slightly stunned.

"What else do you know about her?"

"I know she was a very strong girl, like you," she said. "She wouldn't let anyone push her around, either."

"What else?" she prompted.

"We had both ended up working at the same place in New Orleans. Your mother's uncle owned it," she said. "I was sixteen, a working girl. Your momma was fourteen and a maid, scrubbing floors, washing clothes, cooking, that kind of thing. We got along together and became good friends until your mother's uncle sold out and I had to move on to a new house out west."

Ginger shook her head.

"Those weren't very good times. It seems not long after that she met your father and he brought her here. I Don't know any more details about what happened to her after that, but your Daddy told me she loved you with all her heart. If she could have taken you with her, she definitely would have. But she couldn't. Even if it broke her heart, for your sake, she left you with your Daddy. He loved you as much as she did. He was happy you were staying."

Sugar smiled a bittersweet smile and took a sip of her drink.

"I had no idea anyone around remembered her. Daddy doesn't like to talk about her."

"What I think she would have wanted you to know is if you are not happy with how your life is going, do something about it. When you are ready, take control of your own life and find your happiness. You pick your own man. Nobody can tell you who to love. Don't let anyone lock you up and throw away the key."

"But how will I know when I find the one man I want?"

"Oh, Honey, you'll know," Ginger said.

Sugar felt a weight lift from her heart. She had always dreamed of hearing about her mother but thought she never would. Now, in the short space of an hour, she had a message from her. Sugar felt overwhelmed. Her head started to spin. She put out her hands to steady herself. Too much whisky, she thought.

Ginger helped her stand then hugged her.

"I am so glad you came to me. Please come and visit me often. You remind me so much of Nicolette it's almost like having her here. Please remember, don't tell Quint we talked about your mother. He will be really mad at me."

"I won't," Sugar promised.

Ginger kissed her on the cheek and helped her down the stairs.

"Good-bye and thank you." She hugged Ginger. "I'll be back to visit and make Daddy bring you to the house for dinner soon!"

Sugar rode away on Jonny wishing she had brought Magic after all. She felt like they could catch the wind today.

Sugar still felt a little woozy when she and Jonny trotted into the stable yard both eager for a cool wash and dinner. She felt a sudden puff of cold air hit her lower leg close to her ankle. Strange, she thought, and bent over to see what may have caused it. Suddenly, she heard a gunshot then the whizzing sound of a bullet passing over the back of her head. If she had been sitting up where she was only seconds before, that bullet would be a large hole in her temple, she thought. Instead of sitting up, she let herself fall off the saddle landing face down in the dirt. She lay there, stunned, then tried to get her legs to stand and run. Before she scrambled to her feet, two large hands scooped her up and ran with her into the bunkhouse. Cody set her on one of the bunks and brushed the dirt off of her mouth so she could talk. Just then, the door shattered open and Quint barreled into the room pushing everyone away from her. He grabbed her up and held her in his arms looking her over to see if she had been shot. Fortunately, she sustained no injuries except the scrapes on her head from the fall. He hugged her to him while she cried, shaking so hard she choked trying to breathe through the tears.

Rachel came running and seeing Sugar struggling said, "Quint! Take her up to her room. I'll clean her up."

Quint stood, hurried to her room and laid her out on the bed. Sugar curled into a ball and tried to breathe slower.

She looked up at her father and forced out between deep breaths, "Daddy, someone tried to kill me."

"Don't worry, Baby, Daddy is going to fix this. Don't be afraid." He brushed back her soft black hair and kissed her on the cheek. "Rachel will bring you some supper."

Quint slept little that night. He sat outside Sugar's door with his rifle in his lap wishing the scum who shot at her would come back. He knew exactly where his first shot would go. He could only think of one person stupid enough to try to shoot his little girl and that was Jordan Averill. He'll go to the Sheriff tomorrow and look like a man following the letter of the law to get justice, he thought, but he will not sit around and let anyone take pot shots at his daughter.

Jordan Averill will get his, he swore to himself, and I won't miss.

CHAPTER 5

Quint moved around on the hard wooden chair trying to relieve the ache in his lower back. He had been looking for that comfortable spot all night finally admitting it didn't't exist and never did. At the age of fifty-six having spent as many hours in the saddle as he had, he was lucky he only had a few aches and pains. He thought about how good he felt after one of Ginger's special massages. I wish she was here now, he thought.

He stood slowly, stretching his stiff joints until his legs finally woke up. Not wanting to wake Sugar, he moved as quietly as possible to her bedroom door and listened for sounds of sleeping. He thought he heard her regular breathing. Carefully, so as not to awaken her, he hurried to his room to clean up and get to town early. He wanted to talk to Sheriff Grady Speal as privately as possible then get back home to watch over Sugar.

Sheriff Speal sat at his desk drinking boiled coffee and reading the latest wanted posters that were coming in faster than usual. With the weather warming, more people were moving around outside. Some just needed to get out of the house where they had been shut in all winter. Some had not seen their friends in weeks or even months and needed to catch up on how they made it through.

More people, more problems, Grady thought looking up to see Quint walking through the door. He stood and shook hands with his old friend.

"Quint!" Grady said.

"Hello, Grady," Quint patted him on the shoulder. "Haven't seen you in a while. Doin' okay?"

"Oh yeah," he said. "Pull up that chair over there," he indicated one of the two chairs sitting at a small table.

"Are you busy?" Quint pointed at the stack of posters on his desk.

"No, I can do this any time. I do this when there's nothing else to do." He noticed Quint kept making agitated movements, checking his gun, glancing at the door, looking out the window. "What's on your mind today, Quint?"

Quint looked down at the bare wood floor.

"Family problems," Quint said.

"What's wrong?" Grady knew Quint's only family was himself and a beautiful young daughter that kept him busy keeping her happy and making sure none of the men in town bothered her. He had taken care of that problem when she was just a girl by arranging a marriage for her. He married her off to the son of the family next door. The arrangement seemed more of a business proposition than a love match, but he knew when to keep his nose out of other's business. He never asked about how they were getting along, but he did hear stories from the townspeople. He had expected to have Quint in the office long before now.

Quint looked at Grady.

"You know about Sugar and Jordan being married, don't you?"

Grady nodded his head.

"Yes," he said.

"What I thought was the answer to all my problems four years ago has turned out to be a really bad idea. As a matter of fact, it turned out to be one of the worst ideas I have ever had. Jordan and Sugar hate each other. They have been fighting ever since the wedding and now Sugar wants him out of the house. She keeps asking for me to get her a divorce. I have been telling her to give it some time. But they were fighting, and she kicked him hard on the leg with her boots on. He left for a couple of days and last night, when Sugar was riding to the stable, someone took a shot at her. They missed but not by much."

All the color drained from Grady's face.

"Is she all right?" he asked.

"She was still asleep when I left the house this morning. But she was very upset last night. I sat up in front of her door all night with my shotgun and my Jim 45 on my lap." He ran his fingers through his hair. "But I can't guard her forever. She is a good shot but that's not going to stop a bullet coming from behind. I need your help, Grady. We need to put a stop to this right now."

"You're right," Grady said. "This is scary. Did she get a look at the shooter?"

"No, he was behind her. But who else could it be besides Jordan?" Quint's voice sounded strained as if he might start crying. Grady got up, filled Quint's coffee cup and handed it to him.

Quint took a sip.

"Thank you," he said. He took another sip and rubbed his forehead. "I want this stopped before it goes any further."

"Of course, you're right." Grady said staring straight ahead as if thinking. "Let's do this. I'll ride out to the Rocking A and talk to the Averills. If Jordan is wound up in this, we may have to track him down. You go home and guard Sugar. I am going to wire a friend of mine in Dallas. He heads up a small Texas Ranger platoon. I'll ask him to send someone down to help us. As soon as I get that done, I'll come by to see how you're doing. Sound Good?"

Quint stood and shook Grady's hand. "I really appreciate your help," Quint said.

Quint hurried back to the ranch. He knew Sugar could take care of herself, but he didn't want her to be in a position where she had no other choice. He had hoped she would take to Jordan and settle down and grow roots and never leave him like her mother did him, but the exact opposite was happening. And now she is in danger. Quint tied his horse and ran into the house anxious about his baby girl.

Sugar sat at the large rough-hewn kitchen table drinking coffee and eating eggs and fresh baked bread talking to Rachel while she readied to fix the noon meal for the ranch hands.

"How long were you and Stan married before he passed?" Sugar said in between bites of egg.

Rachel flipped an egg and looked over her shoulder at Sugar.

"Five wonderful years," she said turning back to her cooking.

"What was so wonderful about those years?" Sugar said.

Rachel put her hands on her hips in contemplation.

"It's funny," she said turning and leaning on the stove front. "I don't really remember what we did together, I only remember being with him. I remember the way his brown eyes softened the instant he saw me, the way he reached out to touch me whenever I walked by. He had the funniest habit of pulling the back of my hair when he needed some attention. Wherever we were, he would tug my hair and when I turned around, he would kiss me. I felt truly loved. I knew with him beside me I would be happy no matter what came our way. Now that he is no longer here, I draw strength from all the feelings he had for me and the knowledge that I have been truly and thoroughly loved."

Sugar sighed.

"That's beautiful Rachel," Sugar said and silently prayed that she would find a love like that someday.

"What do I have to do to find someone like that?" Sugar said.

"Just like any girl does. It's like learning to swim. You jump into the water and start paddling." Sugar stood and hugged Rachel. "And be careful you don't drown."

They both laughed.

"Sugar!" she heard Quint call from her empty bedroom.

"In here," Rachael said wiping her tears with her apron.

Quint walked into the kitchen and smiled at Sugar.

"Good morning, what are you two doing in here?" he said kissing her on the cheek and sitting down beside her.

"Girl talk," Sugar said smiling a grateful smile at Rachel.

"Feeling better?"

"I'm fine, Daddy," she said sounding stronger than she felt. "What do you think? Could Jordan have taken that shot at me?"

He knew better than to play dumb. He thought a minute.

"I think the worst thing we could do is jump to conclusions. As things stand now, that shot could have come from anywhere. We have no evidence to accuse anyone."

Sugar's pale blue eyes hardened to an icy grey.

"I know," he said, "Hang on. Getting mad and shooting back's not going to do anything but get us into trouble."

"So, we just let him shoot me?" Sugar said.

"Now, you know I would never let that happen, don't you?"

Sugar looked down.

"Yes," she lifted her head and let a small smile cross her lips.

"That's my Sugar," he said. "I am going to get whoever pulled that trigger on you, but I want to nail them, not get into a game of who shot who first."

He looked at Sugar and she nodded.

"Good," he said. "I've already been to town to see Grady. I explained everything to him, and he understands. He is going to talk to the Averill's today to see what they know before gossip starts and muddies the waters. He's going to tell them if anything happens to you, he's coming for Jordan first."

Sugar thought for a moment. The look on her face softened.

"Sound like a good start?" Quint said.

"Yeah," Sugar said and stood. "I don't want him around here, though. I don't trust him."

"That's what Grady is telling him today," Quint said. "He is telling him and his parents to stay away from us until we find out who's responsible for that gunshot yesterday."

"Okay, but I'm wearing my gun when I'm outside."

"Sounds fair," Quint said.

"I better get busy. That fence around Rachel's vegetable garden isn't going to build itself," Sugar said.

Rachel laughed and winked at Quint.

"That's the stone-cold truth," she said. "I'm not planting until it's up. Too much work planting all that food only to have the rabbits and chickens eat it all. You better get that done today, Missy."

"Yes, General Strom," Sugar saluted. Rachel shooed her out of the kitchen with an angry looking spatula swinging over her head and Sugar laughing all the way.

Someone had already plowed an eight by twelve-foot plot of soft black dirt and left off a bundle of supplies consisting of a roll of six-foot chicken wire fencing, a stack of seven-foot cedar posts, and twelve small boxes of nails.

This won't take long, she thought and got busy laying out the posts.

Four hours later, a dirt covered, sweat drenched Sugar walked around the new fence testing each post for stability and strength. She stood back admiring her work when Cody rode up.

He dismounted and walked the perimeter of the new garden. "You did this?" he asked Sugar.

"Yup," she said.

"By yourself?"

"Yup." She stared into his hazel eyes daring him to come up with a criticism.

"This is nice." He sounded surprised.

"I know," she laughed and watched him walk around again. "Are you planting a garden?"

"No. Rachel has been wanting a garden with a fence for some time now. We've had the materials, but nobody had the time to do it. I thought I'd go ahead and try my hand at it today."

"That was really nice of you." Cody smiled at her, then took off his hat, looked at the sun and mopped his forehead. "Hot," he said putting his hat back on.

"I thought I'd treat myself to a swim at the cove," Sugar said lifting her hair off the back of her neck.

"Want some company?"

"Sure," she said." I'll go get Rachel and show her the garden and meet you back in the kitchen. We can get some lunch and take it out to the cove with us." Sugar felt excited to have something fun to do.

"Great idea," he sounded pleased, too. "Meet you there."

Rachel loved the garden. She packed them a lunch of chicken, fresh bread and butter, cinnamon raisin sweet bread, and a bottle of red wine with two glasses.

As soon as they got to the cove, they stripped down to swimming clothes. Cody wore his jeans and Sugar wore her camisole and jeans. They left their socks and boots and shirts draped over a cluster of scrub bushes on the bank of the pond and dove in. The water felt cool in spite of the afternoon sun. Sugar floated around on her back while Cody splashed around and practiced diving into the deeper end of the inlet. Sugar climbed out first and stepped behind the bushes where she had left her clothes. She removed the soaked camisole and hung it on a sunny branch then slid her arms into her dry shirt. When she came out to set up the lunch basket, Cody walked up the bank and pulled his dry shirt over his head.

"That felt so good," Cody said sitting down beside the food Sugar had spread out on a blanket.

"Didn't it?" Sugar agreed combing through her hair with her fingers. She picked up a napkin and put some of the chicken and bread on it.

"M-M-M," she said taking a bite of her food. She poured each of them a half glass of wine.

Cody took his. He took a sip and puckered his lips.

"I'm not much of a wine drinker," he said smacking his lips like a fish sucking for air.

"You aren't used to it. It takes a while to settle on your palate, about the second glass." Sugar gave him an air toast.

Cody choked down the sour liquid and set the glass upside down on the blanket. Sugar held out the bottle to pour him another. Cody shook his head.

"No, thanks. One was plenty," he said.

They laughed.

Sugar felt herself relaxing in Cody's company. Something about the casual way he moved, talked, seemed to emit a strength of character that slowed the world to a manageable speed. He is a good friend, she thought.

"Think we better get back?" he said gathering the remnants of their lunch and dropping them into the basket. "Your dad is going to be looking for us."

"I'm sure Rachel told him I was with you. He won't worry." She stood and looked at the cove. She felt so safe and comfortable here. She hated to leave, but Cody needed to get back. Reluctantly, she tied the basket to the back of her saddle, and they headed for home.

Once there, Cody rode into the bunkhouse stable and Sugar took Magic into his stall, filled a bucket and washed him down with some soap and a chamois. He tolerated the washing, but the brushing made him lift his muzzle and sing out an appreciative "nay!" Sugar brushed him all over until he shined like molten pitch. "You are beautiful," Sugar whispered in his ear and he nuzzled her arm.

Placing the brush and wet towels in the empty water bucket, she carried them to the worktable to be collected, washed and put away.

She felt good and tired when she walked through the front door. She heard men's voices coming from the parlor. She peeked around the open door to see her father and Grady Speal in the middle of an animated conversation. As soon as they saw her, their conversation stopped. Grady stood and smiled then nodded his head at Sugar. Quint stood and rushed over to her and led her to a large, overstuffed chair.

"Hello, Sheriff," Sugar said. Grady and Quint had been friends for as long as she could remember. They arrived about the same time Granbury started becoming a town. Less than one hundred people had claimed their packet of land when they had braved the elements and Indians to establish the budding town of Granbury. It grew up on the plains just below Comanche Peak and beside the rushing waters of the Brazos River.

"You two talk. I'll go get us something to drink," Quint said and hurried to the kitchen.

"How are you doing today?" Grady said.

"Fine. Nervous."

"That's understandable," he said. "I have some questions about the incident if you feel like talking about it."

"Sure." She tucked her feet up under her and waited for Grady to start.

"All right, about what time did this shooting take place?"

"It must have been around four o'clock in the afternoon. I had been at the Social Club talking with Ginger."

"Do you go to the Social Club often?" he said.

"No, I had a personal problem to discuss with Miss North."

"Does your father know you are consulting with Miss North?"

Sugar let her feet slide to the floor and sat up straight in her chair then smiled her perfect Sugar smile.

"Like I said, Sheriff, I had a personal problem, not a public forum problem."

Grady laughed.

"I know what you mean, the only way to keep a secret is to not tell anyone."

Sugar laughed then looked at the door that led to the kitchen. "Excuse me, Sheriff. I had better go check on Daddy. He has no clue where Rachel keeps the glasses or the whisky for that matter. I'll be right back."

Grady nodded his head and sat back on the couch.

Sugar found the kitchen empty, but a tray sat on the wooden table holding a bottle of whiskey, three glasses, and a plate of sliced pickle and boiled egg on sweet bread.

Sugar lifted the tray and set it down on the dining room table.

"Won't you please join me, Grady," she said indicating the chair across from hers.

"Can I get you anything before I sit down?"

"No, this is very nice," Grady said taking the drink Sugar had poured for him.

Quint walked into the room and joined them at the table.

"Looks delicious. Did you two talk?" He looked at the Sheriff. Grady shook his head no.

"Sugar's not ready yet. She needs to organize her thoughts and get back to me. I'll check in with you tomorrow."

Grady downed the whisky, popped a sliced egg and pickle in his mouth and left.

CHAPTER 6

*J*im Parker tied his horse to the hitching post in front of the Cattlemen Saloon and walked inside holding his head up and both hands on his two Colt 45's, one on each hip. Of average height at five feet ten inches tall, he carried his muscular frame like a taller man telegraphing to on lookers that he had a big attitude and was ready to prove it. He wore his black trousers snug with a chambray shirt and brown leather vest, gray Stetson and tan boots. Today he wore his Stetson pitched forward and squared up like he was locked and loaded and ready to fire. That way people knew that if they messed with him, they would have their hands full.

Parker, as he called himself, sometimes entered situations when he found a disguise helpful. This job required a hard-nosed gun for hire to protect a young woman from a possible murderer. He decided his gunslinger persona would be the best way to go this trip. He would sit around the town watering hole and look tough for a few days.

That way he could get some attention, stir up some talk, learn who in the town might fit his suspect profile.

A member of the Texas Rangers for the past four years, he had handled two successful bodyguard assignments which made him a bodyguard expert in this loosely knit organization. Actually, the Rangers were not an official organization at this time. They had been disbanded for lack of government funds. Until new funding came through, they compared more to private agents, hiring out for various assignments like helping town law enforcement catch a persistent bandit or an errant embezzler. Most of the members served under retired military officers like they had fought under in different conflicts such as Indian uprisings or fort patrol reinforcements. They were disciplined and hardened fighters filling an important role out in an undisciplined part of the country.

Only the second day on the job and Parker already had rumors circulating throughout the town. The generally accepted one said that Quint Wylie had hired a gun slinger to come and take care of whoever had been shooting at Sugar. The rumor wasn't too far from the truth except Parker worked on the side of the law and he had no intentions of shooting anyone unless absolutely necessary.

Sounds busy, Parker thought hearing the loud talking and laughing even before he walked through the swinging doors of the saloon. A large bar ran the width of the back wall of the open room with tables and chairs set for four people each, but the patrons felt free to rearrange them to accommodate any number required. Bar to ceiling mirrors doubled the amount of shining light from the many lighted lanterns along the walls and hanging from the ceiling, and colorful paintings of some of the more notorious ladies of the establishment gave the roomy meeting hall a festive look.

Parker fought his way to an open seat. He rarely entered a saloon full of pretty women without having two or three follow him to his table and this evening, as busy as it appeared, was no exception. His sandy blonde hair and deep blue bedroom eyes made him hard to ignore, even in a crowd.

And even though he needed to work, he never turned down the attentions of a pretty lady.

"Hello," he greeted each one. "Join me. Have a seat. Would anyone like a drink?"

They all said yes. Parker bought two bottles of whisky at the bar, helped himself to four glasses and returned to the table.

"Here you go, Ladies. Help yourself. I'll be right back." He tipped his hat and looked around for another table.

His gaze scanned the crowd then he saw her. The most beautiful woman he had ever seen sitting alone sipping whisky and staring into her glass unaware of the gaiety around her. Parker's evening brightened. He twisted and turned his way through the crowd to her table.

Sugar felt a shadow move over her and looked up. She couldn't be sure about what he said with all the noise, but he looked like he wanted to sit down.

"Sorry," she shook her head no. "I'm waiting for my father. He'll be here any minute." She looked back down.

Without thinking, Parker reached out and placed two curled fingers under her chin and lifted her face up to his. Before he could take his next breath, Sugar jumped out of her chair and held her .36 drawn and pointed directly at his heart.

Parker froze. He held his hands away from his guns.

"Whoa, whoa, whoa!" He yelled and stood perfectly still; his muscles coiled ready to dive under a nearby table if she moved.

Sugar's steady hands and cool grey eyes locked on Parker's handsome face, ready to pull the trigger at a moment's notice.

The partiers froze in place ready to duck if Sugar opened fire in these close quarters.

"Sugar, no!" she heard her father's voice break through her panic.

Quint fought his way to her and gingerly took the gun from her hands.

Everyone breathed a sigh of relief and talked in a low mumble that returned in minutes to the dull roar of before.

Quint righted her chair and helped her sit and take a sip of her drink.

Sheriff Speal took Parker by the arm.

"Come on," Grady said pulling him toward the door. Parker looked confused but followed along.

Quint waited for the crowd to settle, then led Sugar out the door.

Grady let go of Parker.

"Are you all right?"

Parker looked at Grady.

"Who was that?" Parker said letting out a combination chuckle and sigh of relief. "In my four years as a Ranger that was the most intense standoff I've ever had. And I've dealt with some nasty fellows."

Grady opened his office door wondering what he was going to think when he told him.

"That, my friend, is Sugar Wylie. And that was her father that saved your skin. Her father calls her Sugar, but that's not because she's sweet. Most people in town call her Wildcat because they don't ever want to tangle with her. Now you know why."

"I sure do," he laughed. "She is quick on the draw."

"I've never known her to draw on someone like that. She's feeling the stress of her situation. That's why we sent for help. An unhappy arranged marriage is rapidly growing into a dangerous family feud. Someone already took a shot at her."

"Ah," Parker said. "That's why she's so jumpy. I touched her on the chin. Evidently, she doesn't like to have her chin touched."

"I would advise you not to touch her at all. Her father has taught her to protect herself. She is good with a gun and she knows how to fight with her hands. She's not a small woman. I've seen her get a man off balance and knock him on his rear end in no time. She has a mean upper cut. She'll jump into a man's stomach and throw that upper cut into his gut to where he can't breathe normally for a week."

"Lordy, I guess I got off light," he said feeling lucky.

"Just remember, she has claws."

Parker nodded.

The office door opened, and Quint and Sugar walked in. Sugar immediately looked at Parker and began to apologize.

"I am so sorry Mr. Parker. I had no idea who you were or what you wanted."

"Don't worry, Mrs. Averill. I understand perfectly. I shouldn't have touched you."

She laughed.

"Better warn me," she said smiling one of her famous Sugar smiles at him.

"You can bank on it," he said.

He looked at Quint and shook his hand.

"Nice to meet you, Mr. Wylie."

Quint bounced a nod at him.

"I need to write up a detailed statement of all the activities that have brought us to this point. This could take a while. I would like to start tonight."

Everyone looked at Sugar.

"I'm ready," she said.

"I need to stay close to town and keep an eye on these trail riders," Grady said.

"Okay," Quint said. "Why don't we ride out to the ranch where we can be more comfortable? Rachel can fix us some dinner. We can work and eat and get this going."

All agreed. Sugar, Quint and Parker saddled up and headed for the ranch.

Afternoon shadows had started to appear by the time the trio arrived at the Double Bar W. They secured the horses and went inside. Hot and dusty, Quint excused Sugar to go to her room and wash up, then guided Parker to the washroom in the bunkhouse. Refreshed, they met back in Quint's study to get started.

Sugar had changed into a cornflower blue gingham sundress with a ruffled neckline and hemline and matching blue slippers. She had twisted her thick black hair and pinned it high on her head.

Parker tried not to stare and had to pretend to stifle a

cough to stop his jaw from dropping. She looked so feminine. She looked so sweet! He had seen Wildcat, now he had seen Sugar.

Parker took his seat behind Quint's heavy maple desk and prepared to write.

"Miss Wylie, please tell me in your own words and as much detail as you can remember, about your complaint that has brought us here today."

Sugar looked around the room then at her father and then back at Parker. She knew if she could start talking the whole story would come pouring out, so she decided to begin at the beginning.

"When I was fourteen years old," she started and in a loud, clear voice she told the story of how she wound up having to dodge a bullet.

The sun had dropped enough to require lighting the lamps in the study. Rachel moved in and out silently while they worked.

"Mr. Quint, I have dinner prepared if you are ready for me to set the table."

Everyone's eyes looked swollen and only half open.

"Yes, please, Rachel," Quint said. "Thank you."

"Yes, Sir," she said and hurried out of the room.

Quint stood first, then Sugar stood and stretched, coaxing the blood back into her hands and feet.

"I'll take your statement next Mr. Wylie, after dinner, of course."

"That will be fine, and you don't have to call me Mr. Wylie. I'm Quint and she is Sugar."

"Thank you, sir. Do you mind if I work at your desk this evening?"

"No. Use it as much as you need."

"I will take you up on your invitation to stay the night if that's okay. I'll find a place in the bunk house."

"Of course. Tell Cody, he'll set you up."

"Thank you," he said.

Rachel came in.

"It's ready," she said. Sugar took Quint's arm and they went into dinner.

After dinner, Parker and Quint returned to the study to talk. Sugar helped Rachel with the cleanup in payment for making her a nice hot bath and retired to her room to prepare.

Parker sat at Quint's desk to continue transcribing his notes.

Quint sat in the comfortable chair in front.

"Cigar?" Quint offered.

"No, thanks," Parker said.

"Brandy?" Quint said.

"No, thanks. Delicious dinner, thank you."

"Glad you enjoyed it."

"Can we talk a minute?" Quint said.

"Sure."

Parker put his pencil down and looked at Quint.

"I'm worried about Sugar," Quint started. "She is in danger right now. I need someone capable of protecting her day and night. I would pay a reasonable wage plus a room in the house with meals. Would you be interested in that job?"

Parker sat back in the chair. That's not such a bad idea, he thought. He was going to be watching her anyway, this would make his life easier. He could use the money. But he would have to be careful and not get too involved with her. She was the kind of woman who could make a man forget what he was supposed to be doing.

"Yes, I would," he said.

"Fine, then," Quint sounded pleased. "I may have to leave town in a few days. I will expect you to stay with Sugar every waking minute. It would be best to stay inside, but I can't see Sugar doing that. She's headstrong but do whatever you have to do to keep her safe."

"Yes, Sir. You can count on me," Parker said.

"Work as late as you want. I'll see you tomorrow."

"Yes, Sir."

Parker listened as Quint walked to his bedroom, stayed for a few minutes, then exited by the back door. A few minutes later, he heard him ride away. He made a note in his new journal.

Guess I better go get a bunk lined up for the night before they're all taken, he thought. Still tired from the night before, he left his notes from his Sugar interview on the desk and went out to the bunkhouse to find some rest.

Sugar climbed out of the bath and slipped into her pink nightgown. That was heaven, she thought stretching for the ceiling. She walked slowly around the room and turned down the lights. The soft covers felt fresh and cozy on her warm clean skin. She listened for a minute wondering if Parker still sat working at the big wooden desk. She closed her sleep heavy eyes and imagined his muscular arms wrapped around her. For a minute she thought she heard light footsteps outside on the back porch, then her head sunk into her soft pillow and she drifted off to sleep.

CHAPTER 7

He walked softly down the side of the house stopping for a quick peek through the sheer curtains.

The vision in the bath froze him in his tracks.

Keep moving he yelled to himself, but his body refused to go. His mind slowed. A dull buzzing hummed in his ears.

This is a dream, he thought.

He could see himself stepping into the bath with her, watching the glimmering drops of water run down the perfect breasts to shimmer on the tip of a rose-colored nipple before dropping tauntingly onto a soft beckoning patch of curling black hair and disappear teasingly out of sight.

He wished he could follow that drop.

He felt himself moving, growing hard with desire that whispered, she wants you. The windowpane rattled when he reached out to open the window. He had just enough time to duck under the sill out of sight before she looked up. He trailed his fingers along the rough-hewn rock on the side of the house until he reached the awning over the back porch.

He had lost track of time. He had forgotten where he was.

Then in the dim light from the kitchen window he saw the men's dirty work clothes and boots piled under a wash sink near the kitchen door.

He smiled and gathered the items into his arms like he had found a treasure and melted into the shadows with a silent laugh.

CHAPTER 8

*O*h, my goodness, Rachel said fanning her face with her hand as she shuffled into the kitchen and lit the lantern for her morning walk to the hen house to gather eggs for breakfast. What is that awful smell? She wondered collecting the wicker basket with the large handle she used to carry the eggs back to the house. Lifting her shawl from the hook by the door, she draped it over her shoulders then opened the wooden door. She unhooked the screen door and stepped out on the back porch.

A wave of foul air immediately engulfed her. She dropped the basket on the porch floor and covered her nose and mouth with her hands.

"Have mercy!" she yelled then hurried back into the house and slammed both doors.

"What is all this noise?" Quint hurried into the kitchen and helped Rachel sit down to catch her breath.

"There's a terrible smell out on the porch, like something died," she said.

Quint wetted a dish cloth and handed it to her then walked to the door and stepped out shutting the door behind him. The screen door slammed shut. He looked around for what could be causing the smell when he saw the white object about the size of a small dog swinging from a rope. Quint looked closer to see a suckling pig with numerous slashes across its body. A large knife with a thick curved blade pinned a note to the carcass' chest' Someone had butchered the poor creature and cut its mouth into a gapping grin making it look like some ancient pagan god of death, Quint thought.

"What the---" Cody said from behind Quint staring at the gruesome object on the wall. "I'll get it down," he said and ran off to the barn for a ladder and tools.

Quint looked at the note.

One word had been hand painted in blood: Sugar.

Quint let out an angry growl and jumped up and tore the fetid message off the wall.

Cody let the ladder fall to the ground and jumped onto the porch.

Parker came running behind Cody.

"Don't destroy that note," he called. "That's important evidence."

Quint looked at the paper in his hand ready to tear it into a thousand pieces. He hesitated then handed it to Parker. "Here, put this away," he said. "Let's get this cleaned up before Sugar sees it."

Just then, Sugar stepped out on the porch.

"What is it?" she asked looking at the mess on the floor. She hadn't taken time to dress. Her light robe fluttered in the morning breeze.

Quint put his arm around her trying to protect her as much as he could.

Sugar braced herself for bad news.

"Someone has sent us another message."

"What? This?" She reached down and picked up the dead pig by the tail. "Somebody butchered a hog?"

Parker took out the sign and handed it to her. She looked at the paper with her name, then looked at the carcass in her other hand. "Okay," she said placing the smelly message back on the floor. She handed the note back to Parker. She leaned against her father and looked up at him with tears shining in her pretty light blue eyes.

"What do we do now?"

Parker spoke up first.

"I'll tell you what we are going to do. We are going to go inside and make a plan. Then we are going to follow that plan and catch this bastard!"

Sugar smiled. "Good Plan."

By this time all of the hands had heard about the threat to Sugar. They ran out of the bunkhouse buttoning up shirts and stuffing in shirttails ready to learn what they could do to help. The small army of twenty-five men, horses saddled, milled around the yard anxiously determined to protect their "Little Sister."

Sugar dressed as she walked not wanting to miss out on the planning. She hurried as fast as she could pulling on her Levi's, work shirt, boots and six shooter. She twisted her hair into a knot and tucked it inside her lucky hat, the hat she wore when the bullet sizzled over her head not through it and ran downstairs to the parlor. She arrived just in time.

"All right, everyone got your assignment?" Quint said.

"Parker, you're coming with me to the Averill's. Gordon, you divide the boys into groups of three and give each group territory to search for Jordan. Stop by and pick up the Sheriff. Tell him what happened and let him do whatever he thinks best for himself or he can join one of us."

When you find Jordan, take him to the Sheriff's Office and guard him until we all meet back there at noon."

He looked around the room.

"Anything else, Parker?" Quint said.

"No Sir," he answered.

"Okay, let's move out."

Quint gave the order, and everyone started for the door.

Sugar watched and listened patiently waiting for her orders, but her father walked past her without realizing she stood there.

She caught up with him and grabbed his shirt sleeve.

"What about me? What's my assignment?"

"Oh, there you are. You have the hardest assignment of all," he spoke in a low voice. "You are assigned to work with Cody making sure you stay safe while we find Jordan."

"That's not an assignment!" she protested and stomped her boot on the carpeted floor.

"Like I said, that's the hardest one of all. Otherwise, Jordan's going to nail your cute butt to the back door to stink up the house." He smiled.

Sugar laughed. "That's not funny," she stood on tip toes and kissed him on the cheek. "I love you, Daddy."

"I love you, too, sweetheart. You mind Cody." He gave her his stern daddy look and walked out the door.

Sugar looked around the room then crossed to the

window. When she saw the men mounting up for the day her heart filled with appreciation. Everyone wanted to do his part and I'm complaining, she admonished herself. How can I help? Surely, Rachel has some chores in the house I can do.

Sugar peeked in the kitchen but found it empty. That smell, she thought, opening the door only to have it waft past her into the kitchen again. Stepping out on the porch, she filled a bucket, added some lye soap flakes and scrubbed the entire porch. The odor improved, but a mushy mess still clung to the porch wall where the carcass had dangled overnight. Sugar dragged the ladder Cody had dropped earlier onto the porch and propped it precariously against the house. Grabbing the handle of the wash bucket, she reached her foot up to the first rung of the ladder.

"Stop," Cody yelled. "Put that bucket down before you kill yourself!"

Sugar let the bucket drop from her hand with a loud "bam!" then turned and let go an irritated sigh. "So, you can scare me to death first?"

Cody softened his voice.

"Sorry. I didn't mean to scare you. But that ladder won't hold on that wet floor and if that doesn't happen, that bucket will pull you off the ladder."

Sugar looked at the scene before her and had to agree Cody made a good point.

She looked back at him and raised her eyebrows.

"Sorry," she said. "I wasn't thinking."

Cody tried not to laugh but failed.

"Give me that bucket," he took it out of her hand and brushed passed her to the ladder. He had no trouble reaching the smelly spot and scrubbed until the soiled wood looked new.

"That looks nice, but you better get down from there before Rachel sees you or you'll be scrubbing this entire porch for the next two weeks."

Cody's long legs made the trip down the ladder in two giant steps and one more to clear the porch. He emptied the bucket of corruption out behind the barn and left the bucket there.

Sugar broke out in laughter at the tough cowboy running like a scared rabbit away from the idea of having to do housework.

It was funny, she thought, how she forgot her problems whenever Cody was with her.

PARKER AND QUINT walked out of the Social Club and mounted their horses to find the sheriff trotting up to meet them.

"Hey Grady," Quint said. "The boys catch up to you?"

"Yes, they did." Grady took off his hat and wiped his brow with his handkerchief then stuck it back in his pocket. "Heard anything about where he might be yet?"

"Not yet," Parker said. "We were just discussing going out to the Rocking A to see if he is there. I need to get their deposition about these goings on anyway. But I told Quint I thought it would be better if he didn't go. That has showdown written all over it. I don't want to escalate the situation any more than it already is," he said.

Grady looked at Quint.

"I'm going to have to agree with Parker on that," he said.

Quint looked at the hard-packed ground for a minute getting control of his temper and looked back up at the two men.

"I guess I can take some time to go check on Sugar, make sure she hasn't talked Cody into helping her do something on her own."

Both men agreed.

"Okay, I'm going home. You fellows meet me there when you finish with the Averills or send someone if you find Jordan."

"Sure thing," Grady said, and the two law men pointed their horses in the direction of the Rocking A.

PARKER WATCHED Arthur Averill step out onto his front porch and aim the Winchester 1866 Repeating Rifle at him. "Hello, Grady." Arthur said looking from one man to the other. "Who's your friend?"

Grady looked at Parker.

"This is Texas Ranger Jim Parker from Dallas come down to help us sort out the problems between you and Quint Wylie."

Arthur watched closely as the men got off their horses and tied them to the hitching post.

"Mind if we come up for a visit?" Grady said.

Arthur kept the rifle on them and said, "Come on up."

Parker walked up the porch steps and over to Arthur with a friendly smile and his hand out for a respectful shake. "Nice to meet you, Mr. Averill."

"Thank you, Mr. Parker,"

"Call me Arthur. And I don't need any help with Quint."

"I go by Parker. And can we come in and talk about that?" Arthur looked at Parker then at Grady. He shouldered the rifle.

"Please come in, won't you?"

He held the door open and they walked into the parlor and sat down.

The house looked like a well-built, single story, Ranch House style with nicer furniture and decorations than most of the people out on a cattle ranch probably had. Doilies covered the surfaces of the occasional tables beside the brightly colored Velvet covered sofas and chairs. A giant floral covered Victorian print ottoman took up the space in the middle of the room giving an impression of old-world charm and grace to the home.

"Please make yourselves comfortable, and I will go find Constance."

A few minutes later, a housekeeper entered the room with a coffee service and poured each one a cup. They each thanked her.

She dropped a short curtsy.

"I hope your day goes well." She smiled and left the room.

"Here she is," Arthur said.

"Nice to meet you Mrs. Averill," Parker said standing and taking her hand for a moment.

"Mr. Parker, Grady, nice to see you."

"How are you, Constance?" Grady said.

"A little upset."

"That's why we came to see you two today," Parker said as they all took a seat.

"We at the bureau were contacted about a developing

feud here in Granbury over an arranged marriage not working out. Is this a problem you are having?"

"I don't need any help," Arthur said. "I have a crazy neighbor attacking my boy, but it's not a problem. I can take care of it myself."

"That's what we are trying to avoid, Arthur," Grady said. "We don't want anyone hurt," Parker said. "We'd rather work this out like the intelligent people we are."

"It's not that easy," Constance said. "There are broken contracts and promises here involving some compensatory considerations. These arrangements were certified and filed in court. The Wylie's are treating this like we have a young, spoiled girl who is not getting her way so we will just renege on all promises and forget the whole agreement. No, that's not how we are going to solve this."

"I see," Parker said and looked at Grady.

Grady shrugged his shoulders and kept smiling.

"Well, that was a great help, thank you for the insight." Parker said standing to leave. "I would like to talk to Jordan. Is he here?"

"No." He began herding Parker and Grady out.

Constance hurried around them and opened the door. Grady turned to look at Arthur.

"When you see Jordan would you please ask him to drop by my office?" His friendly smile had disappeared.

"Yes, I will." So had Arthur's.

CHAPTER 9

Sugar lounged in the big leather chair in her father's study. She found a copy of an old penny dreadful titled, The Lady and the Badman. She had gotten to the part where the Bad Man grabs the Lady and kisses her until she faints. Sugar had never kissed anybody until she felt she had to faint. She closed her eyes and tried to visualize how that would feel.

The front door opened, and she heard her father's voice talking to someone. She straightened in the chair and her father walked into the library with Grady and Parker. Parker looked worried and Grady's face had tightened into a painful looking grimace.

Something's happened, she thought standing and tossing the book in the chair. Quint walked straight to his liquor cabinet and took out his favorite brandy. He poured out four glasses and handed the first one to Sugar.

"What is it, Daddy? What's happened?"

The three men didn't't speak, they emptied their

glasses in one gulp then looked at her. Sugar managed two good sized sips then her father told them all to sit down.

"Where did they find him?" Quint said.

"The old shed behind the new livery stable," Grady said.

Sugar sat very still. "Who?" she said not wanting to hear the answer.

Her father looked at her.

"Jordan. They found Jordan."

"Is he all right?" her voice sounded far away.

"No, Sweetheart, he's not."

"He's hurt?"

"No. He's been murdered."

Sugar's eyes rolled upward, and she collapsed to the floor.

She laid perfectly still for a moment then her eyes fluttered open. Her father's face hovered over her while Rachel flicked cold water in her eyes. Grady held one hand patting like he was making a tortilla, and Parker stood staring looking like he wanted to do something to help but didn't't know what that would be. She smelled like brandy.

"Oh my God," she said, pushing herself up to a sitting position, wiping at the sticky mess on the front of her shirt.

"I can get up," she said. They helped her to her feet, and she wobbled over to the leather chair and fell in with a plop. "Are you sure?" she asked praying there was some kind of mistake.

"I'm sorry, Sugar, we're sure. Quint and I saw him. Evidently, someone ambushed him in the old livery shack."

Rachel, Grady, Parker and Quint watched her for a minute, then continued.

"He looked like someone slit his throat. He's been there for a couple of days." Parker said.

Sugar drew in a loud breath then shook her head as the image of Jordan lying dead in the dirt appeared all too clearly.

"Rachel," Quint said, "please take Sugar to her room."

Rachel walked over to the chair and tried to stand her up, but she wasn't ready to walk.

Cody walked around the chair and scooped Sugar up in his arms. Sugar let him carry her to her bedroom.

"It's going to be okay." Cody spoke softly. "Just hang on. Don't think. Just let things happen. You'll get passed this."

He kissed her cheek and laid her on the bed.

She smiled and mouthed, "Thank You." She felt his arms slide from under her.

Rachel rushed in with some hot coffee and a towel full of ice. "I'll take it from here," she told Cody and shooed him out of the room.

Sugar climbed out of bed and sat in her chair. The coffee tasted good. She felt revived and wanted to go back downstairs, but she really didn't't have anything to contribute. She felt she would be in the way.

"Can I help you, Rachel?" she said.

"Do you feel like it? I need to feed those men and another hand would really help."

"I would like to help you."

"All right. Wash your face and change out of those clothes. I'll be in the kitchen."

Sugar changed into a comfortable floral print calico

dress and joined Rachel in the kitchen. She could still hear her father, Parker and Grady talking.

"Well, I am going to have to ride out to the Averill's to give official notice to them. I am sorry but Sugar is going to have to go tell the undertaker what to do with Jordan as his legal wife. I know Constance and Arthur. They're going to want possession of the body. I don't want to see a fight over the body. Considering the circumstances, you might talk to Sugar about turning over the control of his remains to his parents."

His remains, she repeated to herself in disbelief. She couldn't't let herself imagine what that looked like. How could this have happened? She felt hysteria eating at her composure like a maggot chewing at the remains of a corpse. She screamed and everyone within hearing range ran as fast as they could to her side. She fell to her knees and started crying in earnest now. She cried until she couldn't't breathe anymore, then she reared up and pulled in a ragged gasp of air and fell down crying again, crying like she wanted to force something out, something she had been carrying around inside her for too long. She cried so hard she thought she would turn inside out. Finally, Quint gathered her to him, picked her up and carried her to her bed.

"Go get the Doctor," Quint roared. Seven men jumped up, ran out of the house and thundered away toward town.

"Grady, go ahead and see the Averill's. Tell them Sugar releases Jordan's body to them to do with as they please." He turned back to his daughter crying softly now.

"I'm sorry, Sugar. I never intended any of this to

happen. I'm so sorry." He lowered his head and cried with her.

PARKER OPENED the weathered grey door of the livery shack. Even in the afternoon sun, stepping inside required Parker's eyes a few minutes to adjust to the dark. He lit the kerosene lamp he brought with him and turned the wick up to full strength. The large room jumped to life casting patterns of shadows on the floor, walls and high ceiling. Parker stood in the center of the room and slowly pivoted drinking in every aspect of the crime scene. He had already learned from limited experience that initial subconscious impressions have an interesting way of transforming into flashes of insight later in the investigation. Some called it a hunch. Parker suspected it came from good initial observation, even if the scene had been trampled beyond recognition by curious outsiders.

That done, he picked up a piece of rotted siding and drew out shapes in the dirt of the body and any details he remembered from earlier. The scenario suggested to him that the killer had been waiting inside. He had arrived first to set the scene to his best advantage. When Jordan entered, the killer had a big advantage. His eyes had adjusted to the dark. Jordan's had not. He had seen the room in the light. Jordan hadn't. Jordan thought he knew who waited for him. Maybe he didn't.

Parker took one last look before leaving. Sometimes seeing what isn't there turns out to be as important as what is there. For instance, where is the knife?

He looked his fill, then left.

Thanks to Grady, he had met the undertaker. He

wouldn't have to waste time proving he had access to the victim. Foster Gravis welcomed him and led him into a room where Jordan waited for processing. Perfect, Parker thought. Once again, he performed a thorough visual inspection of the corpse as when first found. Next, he looked for any other trauma besides the cause of death. Finally, he searched Jordan's clothing for any clues. Nothing out of the ordinary in his pants pockets, Parker thought, then reached into Jordan's shirt's breast pocket and pulled out a note addressed to Jordan. Parker slid it into his back pocket. He stopped on his way out to talk to Mr. Gravis.

"Thank you for your help with this matter," Parker said shaking his hand. "Just one more question. Did you find a knife on the victim anywhere?"

Mr. Foster rubbed his forehead.

"No-No never did," he said.

Parker thanked him again and proceeded on his way to the Rocking A Ranch.

SUGAR AWOKE and looked around the room. Everything looked like it did yesterday, she thought, then looked around again. No, something was different, she was sure, but she couldn't't figure out what. Moving slowly, she climbed out of bed. Her entire body shook. She held on to the mattress so as not to fall and followed the edge to the end. The distance to the door looked too wide for her to cross successfully. She stood for a minute, then carefully put one shaking foot in front of the other until the door-knob filled her hand. She stood for another minute, then turned the doorknob and pushed the door open. The door banged against something and Sugar peeked out to see what she hit.

Cody jumped up from his chair in the hallway to see Sugar peeking around the open door facing him.

"Where are you going?" he asked her.

"To find my mother," she said looking at him as if he should have known that. "You can't stop me." Her words slurred together making her hard to understand. She wobbled over, leaned against him and stared into his caring hazel eyes.

"I bet I can," he told her putting his arms around her to keep her from falling. She leaned into his warmth and watched his eyes close and felt his lips move over hers tasting her delicious softness with feather-light kisses until she opened to him with a tenderness that surprised them both.

Cody looked down waiting for her to yell or throw something at least. But she didn't. Instead, she stepped back and blinked twice.

"Do you kiss all the girls who get sad?" she said.

"Only the ones who really need it," he told her. "Come on, let's get you back to bed," he led her back into her room and tucked her into bed. She smiled and held out her arms for another kiss.

"Time to sleep," he told her tucking her arms snuggly under the covers and returned to his chair by her door.

BOOT STEPS SOUNDED on the wooden floor of Sugar's hallway. Cody looked in the direction of the sound. Parker walked toward him at a quick clip.

The day had turned into a long one for Parker and he

felt ready to sit down and take a break. Just one more interview, he thought looking at Cody.

"How's she doing?" he said.

"Mostly she's sleeping," Cody said. "She gets a little restless every so often and takes out walking somewhere. She'll follow you back. No problem. The doctor has her pretty sedated."

"Can you take a break? I need to talk to you about yesterday."

"I can take a few minutes. Can we use a room in this hall? I can hear when she opens the door."

"Is this a room?" Parker opened the door of a small dressing room. "This'll work," Parker said. "Bring your chair." Cody carried his chair to the dressing room and sat down.

"I wanted to talk to you about the trouble here yesterday morning."

"Sure," he said.

"Did you find the pig first?"

"No. Rachel found it first then Quint went out to look at it."

"Exactly what did you see?"

"I smelled it first. A rotten meat smell let me know something rotten hung in the air. Quint came out on the porch and saw it and I ran up and seeing where it was I ran to the barn to get a ladder but, when I ran back with the ladder, Quint already had the carcass off the house and thrown out in the yard."

"What did you do with the carcass when you took it away?"

"I buried it behind the barn to kill the smell."

"Can you take me to it?"

"Sure. We can ask Rachel to come sit for a few minutes on the way out."

"Okay."

Parker followed Cody out to the barn. Cody showed him a built-up spot where he had dug a hole and left the pig carcass. Parker thanked him and Cody returned to his assignment.

Parker took a shovel out of the barn and dug up the pig. It was ripe yesterday. It was rotten today. Parker wrapped it in a tarp and tied it securely. Then he walked the entire perimeter of the barn. At first, he hadn't noticed another patch of fresh turned earth not far from the first. He picked up the shovel and started digging. Just a few feet under he discovered a set of men's clothes and pair of boots and a hat covered in what looked like blood. He didn't't find a knife, but the clothes definitely needed to be identified. He secured the pig carcass in the barn and carried the remainder of the evidence to his room.

It's too soon to start thinking, he told himself pushing back on a feeling that had grown stronger as the day progressed. At least sleep on it, he thought looking up at the slow waning sun. The sudden need for a hard drink and a soft chair sent him in the direction of Quint's study where he planned to stay for a good while.

Sugar opened her eyes and looked around the room. The kerosene lamps had burned out. The air outside the covers felt cold adding to the shivering brought on by the sedative the doctor had given her. She sat up and dangled her bare feet over the side of the bed.

She had been so busy fussing about Jordan she hadn't really considered the final outcome of their fighting, but she never thought about would die.

84

She dragged the satin comforter across her shoulders and wrapped it around herself as best as she could. Now she was looking at a funeral with all his friends and family. She felt like she had a large pit in her stomach. Probably the whole town would be there. The pit grew some larger. Nobody wants to miss out on the gossip sessions happening all over town, she thought. On one hand, she wanted to hide in her room until all this ended, but she didn't't think she could live with herself knowing she had taken the selfish way out. Jordan did not deserve to be murdered like that. She was going to honor his name at his funeral by holding her head up and paying her respects to him and his family, then put an end to this whole affair.

Sugar jumped off of the bed, dressed in her red gingham house dress and slippers and slowly opened her door. Cody slouched in an uncomfortable wooden chair fast asleep.

That's going to stop, she thought walking softly to the stairs that led up to the secret forbidden room she had avoided for too long. She was a grown woman. She wanted to explore the room and she intended to do it. She wanted to learn whatever she could about her mother. I'm sorry for Daddy's pain, but if he cannot bear looking at her things, he doesn't have to look. I am. Sitting around and worrying about what secrets the room holds needs to stop. She pulled a skeleton key from a door and grabbed a low burning lantern off a table as she walked to the store-room. She inserted the key and the lock clicked open. The room looked smaller than she remembered. She turned up the wick on the lantern and a yellow glow spread over the room.

As far as she could see, nothing had been changed since the previous time she had visited. However, she noticed, someone does come in and clean regularly. The carpets were clean and fresh with no dust collecting on shelves or clothes. Odd for a room that no one uses full of belongings no one wants. Also, she noticed on her first visit at six years old, everything looked so glamorous and enchanting. Now, at eighteen, when she looked, she saw out of style dresses and shoes and gaudy costume jewelry. But when she saw the white dress with the glass beads and the silk petticoat and lace overdress, it looked as beautiful and enchanting as the one she had discovered twelve years ago. The wedding dress still hung on its own rack away from the rest of the wardrobe.

Sugar walked over to take a closer look. Nervous at first, she reached out and gently touched the cool silk, ran her fingers over the clear crystal beads, slid her hand under the delicate entwined lace. I wonder if she wore the same size as me, she thought and reached up, unhooked the hanger and held the dress up to her body. At first examination it looked like it might fit. She quickly removed her clothes and put on the different pieces one at a time. She watched in the full-length mirror at the back of the room as she adjusted the lace into place over the silk petticoat and, as soon as she did the untouchable object became a beautiful form fitting dress, exactly her size, as if made just for her. She smiled at herself looking so pretty. In the glow of the lantern light in the darkened room, she felt as though the image her mother smiled back at her. Hadn't Ginger said they looked exactly alike?

She heard a soft whistle then saw Cody in the mirror

standing behind her with a look in his eyes she had never seen before. He started to reach out for her, then stopped.

"You look beautiful," he said putting his hands in his pockets and moving away. "Where did you get that dress?"

"This was my mother's dress, her wedding dress," she said.

"Are you getting married again?" He sounded worried.

"No!" she said emphatically. "No, I am going to choose the next husband if there is one and I haven't found him yet."

"How will you know when you have found him?"

"I have been told by people that have done it that there won't be any doubt what-so-ever when I do. I'll just know."

"Really?"

"That's what they say." Sugar shrugged her shoulders.

She looked at the vision in the mirror once more not wanting to let go of the feeling.

"Do you believe in ghosts, Cody?"

"Nope."

"Me neither," she said looking away from the mirror.

"I'll go down and make some coffee. When you get changed, want to join me?"

"Sure." She still felt the strange sensation that something else in this room awaited discovery. "I'll be there in a few minutes."

CHAPTER 10

*R*achel walked into the kitchen to find Sugar and Cody sitting at the table drinking coffee. Rachel's gaze bore down on Sugar.

"What are you doing out of bed?"

"I couldn't't sleep anymore. The medication wore off."

"Are you feeling better?"

"Not really, but I don't think I will feel better until after the funeral today at the Rocking A."

"You aren't going to that today, are you?"

"Yes, I didn't't love him, but he was a person, he had people who loved him. I need to pay my respects to him even if our marriage was a sham. I'm sorry for what happened to him. Whatever he did in his life, he certainly didn't't deserve that."

"That's true," Rachel said.

"You know you are going to need an escort, don't you?" Cody said.

"If anybody wants to go with me, that's fine. Be outside and ready to go when I am."

"I'll pass the word," Cody said.

Sugar went to her room and Rachel helped her set up her bath. She luxuriated in the warm water and let it soothe mind and body. Rachel brought in a bottle of lavender bath salts and sprinkled them liberally into the water. Sugar washed with her rose water soap then dried and tried to relax while Rachel massaged the lavender lotion into her shoulders and back. Sugar washed her hair with the lavender soap and Rachel arranged it on top of her head then rubbed the lotion between her expert hands and patted her hair gently smoothing down any stray hairs leaving a lovely scent of lavender wafting around her. She needed no makeup on her clear sun kissed skin, thick black eyelashes and her pleasantly arching eyebrows. Just a light dobbing of rose-tinted lip rouge finished her grooming. Rachel selected a black dress to wear, but Sugar switched it for a navy blue with a straight skirt and small bustle in the back. She looked beautiful and Rachael secretly despaired that she was headed for a funeral and not a ball.

Quint and Parker waited for her in the parlor. Quint had the carriage cleaned and polished and the matched bays hitched and ready to take the Wiley's in style to honor Jordan and his family at this sad time. Rachel had baked and wrapped a Shepard's Pie for the buffet table and set it in the boot. They knew they were not welcome to stay, but they wanted to follow all conventions to circumvent any censurable misstep that might be misconstrued for a slight to Jordan. Quint, Sugar and Parker climbed into the carriage and the entourage headed out for the Rocking A Ranch.

· · ·

JORDAN'S funeral procession marched in silence. The mahogany coffin gleamed in the midmorning sun through the glass encasement of the horse drawn wagon that slowly ground its way up the hill where his final resting place awaited his arrival. Arthur Averill walked behind the wagon, his arm around his wife Constance who could only stand if Arthur held her up. She appeared barely lucid, flailing her arms about in the air and yelling out unintelligible rantings every few steps.

Sugar and Quint stood back and allowed the mourners to pass by then took their places at the back of the crowd. As they made their way to the top if the hill, Sugar couldn't't help but think back. She remembered the first time they had met. She and her father and the Averills waited in a restaurant. She couldn't recall which one. They had been waiting for over an hour for Jordan to show up. He finally entered escorting a pretty young woman and both of them had obviously enjoyed several drinks before arriving. He did not apologize for being late nor did he say where he had been. Everyone ordered dinner with a round of drinks while waiting for the food to arrive.

Jordan and the young lady flirted and laughed at their private jokes not saying one word to anyone else at the table. When the drinks arrived, Daddy proposed a toast to Jordan and Sugar. Constance and Arthur looked shocked and Jordan refused to take part. His friend he had brought kept looking daggers at Daddy until Jordan stood, took the lady's hand, and they left before the food arrived. Sugar felt confused. Something embarrassing had just happened and it had something to do with her. Later, when Quint told her about the marriage, he had arranged

for her, she promised herself she would never accept
Jordan as a husband and she never did.

The parents held a wedding. People to this day
remembered the beautiful ceremony. But she had always
maintained to herself that she did not marry Jordan, her
father did. As far as she was concerned, she had not
accepted him in word or deed, and she never would.

She looked at the dour people around her. She looked
at Constance Averill. She looked at Jordan in the box on
the wagon, and looked down at herself and asked herself,
why do I feel so empty? Did I really hate Jordan? Did I
really want to kill him? How would I feel right now if I
had actually done it? Her hands started to shake. What
kind of person would that have made me? she wondered.
A terrible one, she thought. She had spent four years of
her life hating him. Now she didn't't feel hate or anger or
even regret. She didn't't feel anything, except empty. She
kept walking.

She watched the service and heard the testimonies of
his family and friends. The more they expressed their
sorrow and memories of experiences with him, the
emptier she felt. Finally, the service ended. As the pol
bearers lowered the coffin into the grave, Sugar searched
in her heart for some response. She didn't't feel sorrow,
she didn't't feel happy and she didn't't feel free. She felt
numb, and she was going to have to live with that.

Sugar looked around to see where Quint had gone. He
stood talking with a small group of people she recognized
as members of the Texas Pacific Railway Committee. She
didn't't feel like talking so she waited there for her father
to finish his conversation. She turned back around to see
Constance Averill striding toward her.

"There you are! You murderer! How dare you show your face here today! I know you killed Jordan!" she screamed as loudly as she could.

Grady heard the shouting and hurried over.

"Constance, stop screaming. There's no call for that. The Wylie's came to pay their respects."

"They came to gloat," she said and spit on the ground by Sugar's feet. "I want her arrested right now."

Her voice grew louder.

"Her and her father. They worked Jordan like a slave. Jordan took that scrub ranch of theirs and turned it into a top ranch in the state. They would have nothing if it wasn't for him. They murdered Jordan so they could steal our land to add to theirs. Sugar was a terrible wife. She never respected him and constantly pitted him against her father. She is a rabid animal that needs to be put down!"

Cody stepped between Constance and Sugar. Quint and Parker ran over to join Cody in forming a protective barrier between Sugar and Constance's grief induced rantings.

Sugar looked at Jordan's mother.

"Don't say anything, Baby," Quint said.

"I have nothing to say," she said.

Quint lifted her hand and tucked it around his arm to give her support. Grady, Parker and Cody lined up behind her. Sugar turned away and walked slowly toward the carriage.

Everyone held to their own thoughts on the ride home. All things considered, Sugar thought, the funeral had gone as well as could have been expected. Poor Constance.

Once home, Sugar took down the nice silver coffee

service and filled it with fresh brewed coffee. She set out the good porcelain china cups and saucers on the silver tray. Rachel had baked a cinnamon spice cake. Sugar carried each into the parlor and displayed them prettily on the buffet. She fanned a stack of fresh washed napkins on the side of the whole then sat in one of the wingback chairs to wait. Quint joined her. They waited together. Finally, several neighbors stopped by to share their condolences and discuss over cake and coffee how tragic and shocking the events seemed. Sugar felt sure some of them came more to learn some gossip than offer condolences, but most had appeared more gracious than curious, and she felt grateful for their offers of comfort. She knew they came from a place of goodness within them. The afternoon passed easier for their coming.

At the end of the day, Quint, Sugar and Rachel cleaned the cups and saucers and silver service, ate an early dinner and sat in the parlor to let this day slip away.

"Do you feel better now, Sugar?" Quint broke the silence.

"Some," she admitted trying to muster up a smile but failed.

"I know Parker will continue investigating so this episode is not over, but I feel that our part is settled so we can relax some. I'm sure the Averills will enact some kind of civil suit. But that's why God made attorneys, I guess," Quint said.

Sugar smiled. "I guess," she agreed accepting her fate.

"I have a trip to Fort Worth coming up. Are you going to be all right here, or do you want to come along?" Quint said.

"Is it the Railway committee?" she said.

"Yeah, I'm afraid things aren't going so good for Ray Hudson and Company. Rumors are swirling around. Financial trouble. Sounds like they are going under."

"Oh no! Are they going to at least make it to Fort Worth?" Sugar said.

"I sure as anything hope so." He ran his hand through his salt and pepper hair.

"Sounds like you are going to be busy. I don't want to sit around the hotel room. Why don't you take Ginger?"

Quint looked surprised.

"What made you think of that?"

"I talked to her the other day and realized she hasn't been around in a while. I like her. You could use some fun. You have been spending all your time worrying about me."

"It could be nice to have a friend with me."

"Daddy, you don't have to be embarrassed in front of me anymore. I'm a grown woman now if you hadn't noticed. I know all about that stuff."

"Young lady, you better not be messing with that stuff."

"Daddy, I've been married for four years." She teased him with a knowing smile.

"You know what Sugar, I'm too tired for this conversation tonight." He laughed.

"I'm serious. It would be good for you to kick up your heels. You work too hard."

Quint stood and walked over to his little girl.

"Come here and hug your poor old Daddy. I love you, Baby Girl. I was really proud of you today. You looked like a real lady." He kissed her on the forehead.

She gave him a big hug.

"I love you, too, Daddy."

"Good night," he said and headed off to bed. "See you in the morning."

Sugar loosened her waist band of her dress and kicked off her shoes. Her feet hurt. Her head hurt. And she had been missing her old boots all day. Actually, she couldn't remember where she had left them. They'll turn up, she thought hoping that Rachel had gotten around to filling her wash tub. She felt like she needed an extra hard scrub tonight so that she could wake up fresh and clean tomorrow.

Opening her door slowly, she saw the steaming bathtub ready and waiting. She hurried into the room and started pulling off the confining dress she had suffered with all day. No more, she said aloud and gathered the dress and all that went with it and threw it on the floor of her large mahogany wardrobe. I'll burn it tomorrow, she thought and jumped into the bath. That's more like it, she smelled the relaxing fragrance of her lavender soap as she joyfully rubbed the first lathering all over her tired body.

CHAPTER 11

*H*e slid from his hiding place under the back porch and crawled silently down the side of the house to the lighted window with the sheer curtains.

He pulled himself high enough to peek through the corner of the dusty bedroom window.

She sat unaware lost in her pleasure.

The water swirled around her as she soaped her arms, breasts, stomach.

He pushed up onto his haunches to see better, then slipped and tumbled backward into the grass.

He froze and held his breath.

Two figures walked out of the bunkhouse, looked toward the stable and the house then disappeared back inside.

In an instant, he jumped to his feet and slithered around the house.

Muffled hoof beats thumped in a grassy patch, then trotted away.

Soon, soon, he whispered and disappeared into the night.

CHAPTER 12

Sugar woke from her nightmares with a start. She pushed up on one elbow and wiped the hair from her face.

"The first day without Jordan in my life," she said aloud. She didn't know how to feel about that. She had carried around so much anger and resentment since the first time they met, she felt strange without it. Although, as swollen and lethargic as her body felt, she did have a subtle mental lightness that prophesied possible recovery someday. She could build on that, she thought. Hard work would fill that empty spot, that's what Daddy would say. She kicked her covers off and jumped out of bed.

Quint sat at the table drinking coffee and talking to Rachel when Sugar walked into the kitchen. "Good morning," she kissed her father on the cheek and patted Rachel on the shoulder.

"You feeling better?" Quint said pleased to see her smiling again.

"I am, thank you. Are you going to Fort Worth today?"

"Yeah, I need to go. I just don't want to leave you with the ranch for the next few days if you're not feeling well."

"I'm fine. I'm ready to get back to work, the sooner the better."

Rachel handed her a cup of coffee. She sat down.

"Parker is staying at the ranch. I'm taking Cody with me." Quint told her setting his coffee cup down.

"Okay," she said sounding a little hesitant.

"Is that all right with you?"

"Of course, he's so much help around here, but if you need him, that's fine."

"I hope I don't. But if Hudson & Company fails, I may need him to come and pick up a few of the men and bring them back. We could have some work ahead of us."

"I hope not." Sugar said.

Quint nodded and took a final sip of coffee.

SUGAR WALKED to the stable and saddled Jonnie up for the day. Magic whinnied and shook his head at her as if knowing they weren't going for their morning run.

"Sorry, Big Boy, I have work to do. We'll go later."

"Big Boy. So that's his name."

Cody walked up behind her. She stepped back and ran right into him. She turned and he caught her in his arms.

"Gracious, I didn't't know you were there," she jumped back, laughing at herself.

"Be careful," he said holding her for a minute making sure she had caught her balance.

"Thanks, I'm good." She righted her hat and looked at him. "What are you doing?" and why do you smell so good, she thought noticing his sandy blonde hair still damp probably from his morning bath."

"Your father wanted his satchel, said it was in here."

"I heard you were going to Fort Worth with him. Be careful, he'll put you to work." Sugar laughed.

"I know." He smiled back.

"But I thought I could learn about the railway, meet some influential people. Sounded interesting."

"You will. I'm glad you are going except I don't know how I'm going to get the chores done without you."

Cody laughed, and looked at the ground.

"I know, that's why I told Joseph to keep in touch with you during the day in case you needed anything."

"Thank you very much. I won't miss you then." She smiled.

Cody looked back up at her and shook his head.

"Yes, you will," he said softly.

She laughed.

"No, I won't," she said softly in reply and turned back toward Magic. "And his name is not Big Boy."

"I didn't't think so," he said and walked over to a cabinet on the wall and took out her father's satchel, "because horses don't have names."

She turned and watched him leave. "Yes, they do," she whispered.

PARKER CARRIED the last of his notes into his room at the Granbury Hotel. He loved the comfort and convenience of working in Quint's library, however, the arrangement no longer fit his needs. He felt the evidence strongly pointed to the person who murdered Jordan Averill. Until the arrest, he wanted to keep his suspicions to himself. He still had to convince Grady that his theories made sense. The evidence was strong but not as conclusive as he wanted. He needed to find the murder weapon.

Where was that knife? he asked himself over and over. It does exist and it is somewhere, he knows. All he has to do is find it. The murderer killed Jordan with it. The murderer butchered the pig with it and left it in the pig to hold the message in place. So, the knife should have been with the buried clothes at the back of the barn at the Double Bar W. But it's not. Why not? Because he plans to use it again?

Parker made sure he had secured all evidence and notes in a locked strongbox inside a locked closet and locked the door when he left, determined to find that knife today.

RACHEL OPENED every drawer of the big bureau one last time. Finally, she thought, those drawers had needed a thorough cleaning for months. She really hadn't planned on spending so much time on the task, but it needed to be done and he was out of the way in Fort Worth. She decided to go ahead and make the time. They looked so clean and fresh once done. She knew he would be pleased when he returned home. She gathered the used rags and old unwearable clothes she had removed from the messy drawers then looked at the bed. When did she last flip that mattress? she wondered. "Ai me," she sighed and set her bundle down.

Parker returned to the scene of the crime with a shovel and not only looked in every nook and cranny of the old stable, but also sifted through every inch of soft dirt on the ground. No sign of a knife in that shack, he thought.

He rode out to the Double Bar W, took his shovel then trenched the perimeter of the barn and tested for refilled holes ten feet out. The chill of the morning had dissipated, and the climbing sun beat down hard enough to bring on a good sweat. He spiked the shovel into the ground and took off his shirt and hung it on the shovel handle. The bright sun combined with the gleaming sweat gave an emphasis to his muscles making him a very pleasant vision as Sugar rode up from her inspections.

He looked like a mythological god with his weapon, the magic shovel at the ready. She surprised herself with a giggle. She hadn't giggled since the sixth grade.

"Hello," she called out.

"Good morning," he said sounding happy to see her. She had a sexy way about her, an enigmatic smile and come get me look in her ice blue eyes that made him think about gentle breezes and moonlight. That and her delicious figure.

"What are you doing?" she said looking at the holes he had dug.

"Just looking to see if I missed anything," he said.

"Looks to me like you need to cool off," she said taking her canteen from around her saddle horn and handing it to him. His chest muscles rippled as he reached for the canteen. She wondered how those muscles would respond to her touch.

"Thank you." He took a long drink. "Whew, I needed that. A cool swim would be nice."

The top of him looks good enough to eat. I wonder what the rest of him looks like, she thought, and a sensuous smile tipped the corners of her mouth. Maybe today is the day to jump into the water like Rachel said. Give this love thing a try. A naughty thrill tingled between her legs.

"Get your horse and follow me," she said throwing caution to the wind.

Parker grabbed his shirt and ran to his horse.

"Okay, let's go," he said.

She led him to the Sleeping Lady Cove. The wildflowers had bloomed since the last time she had been there. Multicolored petals surrounded the pond and decorated the adjoining areas turning the quiet haven into a mystical garden. Sugar sat down in a patch of buttercups.

"Take your swim," she told him.

"Join me?" he said raising his eyebrows in invitation.

"No thanks," she said. "I'll just sit here and enjoy this sunshine."

Parker sat and pulled off his boots and socks. He threw his shirt over a bush to dry and ran and jumped into the water. It felt invigorating. He scrubbed his face and chest then climbed out shaking water everywhere. He sat down beside Sugar.

He has such a beautiful body, she thought. She reached out and raked her fingers across his chest. She looked into his deep blue eyes expecting to see surprise, but instead, they softened.

Parker smiled.

"Wildcat wants to come out and play, huh? Put those claws up."

She looked confused and pulled her hands away, curling her fingers into her palms.

"Let's see if Wildcat can be gentled."

Slowly, Parker leaned his face closer to hers and teased her lips with his until hers softened in response. He pulled back and looked into her silver blue eyes watching him intently.

He smiled a wicked smile then breathed a low, sensual chuckle.

Sugar wasn't sure she felt comfortable with his familiarity, but in spite of her doubts, an overwhelming curiosity kept her still and waiting.

He combed his hands through either side of hair letting his fingers encircle her face and gently pull her to his and kiss her deeply, tasting her soft mouth, making her lean closer, pressing herself against his warm muscled chest.

He released her and took her hands to help her lie down in the soft grass below. A sudden feeling of losing control awakened her better judgement. She pulled her hand from his.

Parker looked surprised but before he could speak, she stood up. He stood, too.

"We better get back before Daddy comes looking for us," she said walking toward Magic feeding on the grass under the tree.

Parker finished dressing and followed after her.

It had been an interesting experiment, she thought as she swung up into the saddle, but not the earth shattering experience she had expected leaving her even more confused than before.

That evening, Rachel served Sugar and Parker supper in the dining room. Afterward, they retired to the parlor. "Rachel certainly is a good cook," Parker said leaning back on the sofa, relaxing after a satisfying meal. "How long has she worked here?"

"All of my life," Sugar said.

"You're lucky to have her. She seems like a real good employee."

"The best, we love her very much. I guess she is actually a family member now." Sugar said.

"I've been wanting to ask you a question, but I didn't want to sound impertinent."

"What is it?" Sugar said.

"What is your real name?"

"Sugar," she said.

"That's your real name?"

"Yes, Sugar Wylie. That's me," she said. "Why? What's wrong with that?"

"Well, it just doesn't sound like a grown woman's name is all. Sounds more like a thirteen-year-old girl. Doesn't your father find it a little juvenile for you?"

"No, not if it is my real name. I love my name," she said starting to grow annoyed with his insinuation. "Don't you like my name?"

"Like I said, it seems a trifle childish," he said. "It's not your fault, though. It's your father's."

"I don't know what you're talking about." Sugar tilted her head up and looked him straight in the eyes.

"Your father has not done well by you. He is trying to hold on to you by treating you like a child, making you dependent on him for your future, your safety, your legacy. That's why he married you off to Jordan. He knew he could control Jordan and keep you here on the ranch. That is why Jordan is dead. He was trying to take you away from this ranch, from your father. Don't you see what's happening? I don't think you are safe here."

Sugar couldn't't believe what she was hearing. How long had he been in town? Two weeks? And now he has somehow divined that Daddy has evil intentions and she is in danger!

"That's ridiculous," she said. "You don't know anything about us and what is happening in our lives."

"People are talking, Sugar. I've heard some stories."

"People talk! Of course, people talk. They don't have anything else to do. They gossip and embellish and make things up for the fun of having something exciting to discuss, but that doesn't make it true."

Sugar couldn't't listen to this anymore.

"I have to get up early tomorrow. I'm turning in. Good-night."

"Want me to tuck you in later after the house settles down?"

"No, you better not. Since being shot at and having a dead pig stuck to the door, I've been a little nervous. I am sleeping with my gun and I might accidentally shoot first and ask questions later. I rarely miss my target especially when I'm nervous. I'm keeping my door locked just in case. Good-night."

In her room, she undressed and climbed in bed. Flashes of memories of soft kisses kept playing with her mind, but every time she would pull away, not Parker but Cody's face looked back at her.

CHAPTER 13

The front door opened slightly, and a shadow slipped through the narrow opening. He paused to listen to the sound of a sleeping house. Leaving the door ajar, he stepped carefully over the carpeted floors down a hallway and came to a halt in front of a bedroom door.

The hinge creaked slightly as he slipped into the room. Letting his eyes adjust to the dark, he pulled the knife from his waist band.

A large bureau stood against the wall.

He tip-toed over and gently pulled the top drawer open. The knife thumped when it hit the bottom of the drawer. He spread some clothes around to cover it.

A sudden crash came from upstairs.

He quickly closed the drawer and waited until the house grew quiet again then carefully retraced his steps

on the carpet leading to the front door and slid out and
away.

CHAPTER 14

*S*ugar turned down the wick in the small lantern she sometimes carried at night. The house had quieted. She couldn't't sleep with the day's events still vivid in her mind. She needed to move around and decided this was a good time to prowl her mother's room again. She hadn't gone through any of the drawers or closets yet. Memories still waited for discovery, she thought.

The room looked as it had every other time she had visited. Whatever disarray left over from before had been put back in order exactly the same as the first time she had found the room years ago, as if the room wanted to tell her something.

That's just crazy, she thought pressing forward into the quiet room. She looked around trying to heighten her senses to reach out for whatever kept calling her, bringing her back again and again. She walked slowly, eyes wide, silently listening. She reached the back of the room and set the lantern on the windowsill then started toward one of the large bureaus when her foot caught on the rack that held her mother's wedding gown. She felt herself falling, waving her arms wildly trying to break her fall. She wrapped her arms tightly around the cool white dress and hit the floor, dress rack, gown and all crashing down with her.

Stunned for a moment, she laid still and stared at the ceiling. She didn't hear footsteps. No searing pain. No blood gushing. She was all right, she realized feeling relieved until she got to her feet and held out the beautiful white dress torn almost in half, tiny glass beads plinking on the floor at her bare her feet. She opened her mouth to scream, then exhaled instead. There, on the floor, where she had landed, lay a yellowed, age stained once white envelope with the word Sugar written across the front.

"What the--? She whispered and bent down to pick it up. She heard a noise coming from what sounded like her father's room. Not wanting to be caught in the forbidden room, she bundled up the ruined gown, grabbed the lantern and hurried to her bedroom clutching the letter to her heart. She crammed the dress into a lump, threw it on the armoire floor and covered it with a blanket. She opened the bottom drawer of the bureau and buried the letter under some old pantaloons, then jumped in bed. She thought she heard muted footsteps on carpet then a door clicked shut. She lay still for some time thinking about her afternoon with Parker. He was really nice to look at and he obviously knew how to make a girl enjoy a moment's pleasure. But nothing felt special about him. He certainly didn't seem to find anything special about her.

He doesn't even like my name, she thought drifting off to sleep. Doesn't matter. I don't have a wedding gown anymore anyway.

She awoke late the next morning, jumped out of bed and dressed for work. The sun rode high in the sky and Joseph had already saddled Jonnie and left her at the back door. Sugar ran out and headed off to work. She felt bad about being late but Buck, Lance and Charlie had already herded two of the six groups of thirty-west steers to water. Kenny had the early spring branding set up and waiting for the calves to arrive. Joseph had four groups of maintenance workers assigned. And a bright spray of sunshine burst over the eastern sky. Looks like a beautiful new day, Sugar thought, and headed back to the house for a late breakfast.

THE BRIGHT MORNING sunshine lit up Quint's room nicely Parker thought as he slowly opened the bedroom door. The hinge let out a slight creak but not enough to disturb anyone, he thought and walked to the center of the room. He looked around to see if anything appeared out of place or as if it didn't't belong there. Nothing stood out.

He walked over to the huge armoire and opened the ornately carved doors. He gave a quick pat to the clothes, held them back and inspected the floor then closed the doors.

Next, he crossed to the large bureau and opened the bottom drawer, tossed the clothes inside and shut the drawer. He repeated tossing each drawer, none having what he expected to find until he reached the top. He opened the drawer and dug both hands into the socks and under shorts, but this time felt a hard, cold metal object on the bottom. He wrapped his fingers around what felt like a handle and pulled the object out into the light. And there it was. The murder weapon, the knife that had slit Jordan Averill's throat.

Solved my first murder case! He wanted to yell but didn't want anyone to know yet. He closed the top drawer catching a wedge of a sock toe in the process. He took a closer look at the knife. He didn't't see any visual evidence of blood. It had a thick curved blade and a carved ivory handle that had been polished to a warm syrup colored glow. He tested the blade and a thin line of red blood swelled out of its path. Beautiful, he thought turning it around and back and forth in his hands without a single thought about Jordan Averill. He heard the backdoor close. Quickly, he grabbed the sock toe sticking out of the drawer and stuck the knife inside then secured it in the waistband of his pants. He pulled his shirttail over the hilt and hoped that covered it. He walked out of the room and closed the door.

He needed to secure the knife, he thought. Leaving through the front door, he jumped on his horse waiting outside where he had left it and headed toward the hotel.

SUGAR STOPPED AT THE STABLES, unsaddled Jonnie and led her in out of the sun. she had worked hard today so she gave her an extra handful of oats and plenty of water. She left her happily enjoying her meal.

Outside, she saw Rachel in her yellow cotton house

dress, white apron and muddy boots bending over some rows of precisely formed soil, dropping seeds every few inches, then gently covering them and sprinkling them with a loving drink of water. Sugar smiled. She looked so happy working in her garden, Sugar didn't't want to disturb her. She continued on in the back door to wash up.

The water felt good on her neck, Sugar thought as she finished washing her face in the wash bowl she had brought to her room from the kitchen. She picked up her dirty Levi's and work shirt and took them to the wash table. She threw the dirty wash water into the back yard and set the pan out to dry.

What's for lunch? she started to consider when she heard several horses running hard into the back yard. Sounds like trouble, she said to herself and hurried to the screen door to look out. Covered in dust and looking like he hadn't slept for days, Cody strode up, removed his hat and said, "Bad news."

Sugar opened the screen door to let him in.

"No thanks, I'm going to have to clean up first."

Sugar stepped out.

"What is it?" Her eyes shone a bright silver in the sunlight.

"Hudson and Company filed for bankruptcy yesterday," Cody said. "All construction shut down six miles west of Dallas. The Committee raised some money, enough to take the supplies on site and finish the job, but the land grant requires that the railway track must reach Fort Worth in two weeks or the state legislature will withdraw the land grant and cease all construction."

Sugar shook her head.

"So, what's the plan?"

"Your father sent me here to get some men to join up with us at Eagle Ford and we'll lay the final twenty-nine miles of track into Fort Worth. It's going to be tough, but we are determined. Volunteer work crews are gathering from towns all over the state."

"Okay, take whoever will go. We'll do our best to maintain here. We can do the bare minimum until you all return. I can handle this."

Cody smiled.

"You're the best," he said and patted her shoulder.

"I know," she said smiling playfully and patted him back. "You go clean up and get some rest. I'll put together some traveling food and supplies enough to get you back to Eagle Ford. Rachel and I will feed you dinner and you can get back on the road."

"Sounds good."

"Okay. Let's get busy."

Cody stood there like he wanted to say something more, then put his hat back on and left.

Sugar ran out to the garden to get Rachel. She explained the situation about the railway, and Rachel jumped right in.

"I'll start cooking," Rachel said and headed for the kitchen.

Cody selected fifteen of the strongest, hardest working men on the ranch and they agreed to go along especially since Quint told Cody to tell them he was paying double their wages if they did.

Sugar thanked them and told them to take their bedding from the bunkhouse and any toiletries they wanted. She selected three strong work horses to act as pack horses for kitchen gear, extra blankets and four large bags of beans, several canisters of homemade jerky, and cornbread fixings to go with the beans. They would have water at the site, she assumed, so they could live on that to start, at least. They could replenish in the towns along the way. As a final gesture of support, she added two bottles of Quint's favorite whisky to make the trip a little easier.

Sugar and Rachel spent most of the afternoon packing. They cooked a ham and 5 chickens with boiled potatoes, gravy and fresh, baked bread. Rachel had two apple pies already made so they set them out for dessert. It looked like a feast when they put it on the table.

Sugar felt sure the men would like to eat alone, but when they came in, they refused to eat until the ladies took their seats. Sugar sat on one side of the table and Rachel sat on the other.

The men seemed in high spirits and told funny stories about happenings on the ranch. The food that had looked like a feast before disappeared fast. They attacked the pies like hungry boys that hadn't had pie in a while. They all ended up in the parlor, each with one of Quint's fancy cigars and a glass of his favorite brandy. The party grew more and more quiet as time to leave loomed nearer.

Sugar and Rachel looked at each other and finally stood to say good-bye.

Cody stood.

"I want to thank these beautiful ladies for their fine dinner and pleasurable company." He raised his glass of brandy and all the men stood and lifted their glasses. Each one shook Sugar's and Rachel's hand and thanked them personally for the delicious supper. Each man set his glass on the table and exited through the back door.

Cody lingered, saying good-bye to Rachel. He watched as she began collecting glasses and carrying them to the kitchen. He turned to Sugar and reached out for her hand. Instead of shaking it, he held it softly then turned it over and raised it to his lips for a lingering kiss. He looked into her eyes then let go.

"Stay safe," he said and followed the others out the door.

Sugar turned to watch him go. Rachel had come back in the room holding a tray and stopped at the table. She watched him go then looked back at Sugar.

"What?" Sugar said to her.

"Nothing," she replied and turned her attention toward the dirty dishes.

With the house silent for the first time since she awoke this morning, Sugar thought of her unread letter waiting in her drawer. I need to go read it, she thought then corrected herself. No, I want to go read it, I need to help Rachel clean the dining table and kitchen. Reluctantly, she found a tray and started clearing dishes.

Two hours later, she fell into her bed without changing her clothes. She smelled like horses and fried chicken.

"Phew!" she said then let her head flop into her pillow and immediately passed out from fatigue.

An hour later, her door opened, and Parker creeped over to the bed.

He reached out and grasped her shoulder.

"Sugar," he whispered giving her a soft shake.

She didn't respond.

"Sugar," he said aloud and shook her again.

"Sugar's not here. Go away," she mumbled.

Parker leaned down to kiss her then stood up again instead.

"Phew!" he said rubbing his nose and left the room.

CHAPTER 15

*Q*uint climbed out of the newly purchased wagon and looked around the staging area. Hundreds of men from diverse walks of life from all parts of Texas had answered the call for help to save the dream of a railway that would allow the large expanse of the sprawling state grow into a cohesive whole ready to open for business with the rest of the country. For the first time since he heard he would be a father, he actually felt excited. Standing on the precipice of the future, he felt energized by the realization that if all of them working together could actually get this rail laid, they would witness the dawning of a new era in this new country.

Quint's heart swelled with pride.

All we have to do is organize the workers, distribute materials, coordinate implementation, and execute according to plan. As he thought about the daunting scope of the endeavor, he looked at the scene of chaos before him, and his enthusiasm came face to face with reality. He took a deep breath and returned to earth still determined to not give up until he had tried to his next to last breath to make the dream come true.

We have two weeks, he thought, how could this not happen? he asked himself then walked to the prearranged spot where the officers of the Citizens of Texas and Pacific Railway Committee would start this train running again.

SUGAR AWOKE the morning after the impromptu dinner fully dressed and smelling like last night's trash pile. Not even stopping for coffee, she wrestled the bathtub into her room and filled it with water she heated from the stove. She stripped off the offending clothes she had slept in and standing on a clean towel, she rubbed her skin red with a preliminary head to toe scrub. Then she stepped into the warm water luxuriating in the feel of lavender scented soap suds soothing her skin and washing her clean.

"Ah-h," she moaned as she stepped out of the bath feeling like a new woman. A vigorous towel buffing removed the excess moisture from her hair and body. She stood naked brushing her hair then rubbed her arms and legs with lavender scented cream to eliminate any lingering odors she may have missed. She then dressed in fresh Levi's and a cotton blouse that Rachel had washed so many times it felt like velvet on her clean skin. While pulling it over her head, she stopped and looked at her right hand softly running the fingers on her left over the spot where Cody had placed his kiss last night. She closed her eyes and conjured up the feel of his soft lips pressed against that sensitive spot in the center. She remembered the night in the secret room when he thought she was too sedated to notice that he had stolen a kiss so sweetly. But she wasn't. He has beautiful soft lips, she thought. Some might mistake his hesitant actions for a tendency toward shyness, but Sugar wouldn't agree. She perceived the feeling more akin to reverence or respect. She longed to see him today. Days always seemed more fun with him around, but disappointment tempered her dreamy musings. He wouldn't be back for two weeks, she thought as the sizzle of her wistful morning fizzled to a halt.

PARKER SAT in his hotel room looking at all the evidence he had gathered in the Jordan Averill investigation. He spread it out on the bed and surrounding floor area to help him figure out the timeline of the crime. He needed to work up a theory of how the crime occurred with a timeline of events shown by the evidence collected, he thought.

The note in Jordan's pocket probably holds first place for the most damning piece of evidence. He considered the obvious proof with biting sarcasm. He would read the letter he found in Jordan's pocket. This letter puts the killer himself right in the middle of the crime scene.

A slaughtered pig nailed to the back porch with his daughter's name on it will rivet the jury's attention on Quint.

And the story of how he found the knife will seal the deal on Quint's guilt, he thought.

Perfect, he thought setting down the closing comments he planned to speak at Quint's trial.

I'm ready, he thought, relieved to have the ground

work finished. He wondered if the pretty little redhead and her friend he had met at the Social Club the other night would care for some breakfast and fun. He'd best go see, he thought, leaving the evidence out on the bed, he walked out the door.

SUGAR WALKED into the kitchen to see Rachel still cooking breakfast for the men.

"How do you feel this morning?" Sugar asked her.

She looked at Sugar.

"How do I look?"

Her face appeared a little swollen and her eyes had a decided droop about them. She looked tired, Sugar thought.

"I don't feel as bad as I look," she said, "I think I stayed in the sun too long working on the garden yesterday." She smiled.

"Probably, but you'll get used to it," Sugar said. "I am going to town later. I'm going to look for a sunbonnet for you."

"Thanks," she brightened. She dished up two fried eggs and toast and handed it to Sugar. She poured her some coffee then returned to cooking.

"I've been meaning to talk to you about something." Rachel said.

"Oh?" Sugar said.

"It's about Parker."

"What's he up to?" she asked.

"I don't know, but I am afraid it's not good."

Sugar frowned.

"He has been going in and out and he seems to be

looking for something. And he is not sleeping here anymore. I looked in his room yesterday and he has moved his clothes out. I think he is staying somewhere else and doesn't want us to know."

Sugar waited for her to go on.

"Two mornings ago, I cleaned and straightened out your Dad's room. I sorted out the old items from his drawers, then freshened and flipped the mattress."

"He will be happy about that," Sugar said.

"He is gone so I thought I'd get it done."

"Thanks," Sugar said.

"But that afternoon Parker came in and messed up every drawer, turned your father's mattress back over, and left. What do you think he might be doing?"

Sugar thought a minute.

"Sounds like he's looking for something."

"That's what I thought," she said shaking her finger at Sugar. "What would he be looking for around here?"

"I don't know," she said, "but I'm going to find out."

She stood.

"I'm going to find him. I'll be back later." She hugged Rachel and left. On her way out of the house she stopped by her room, took her gun belt off its hook in the armoire and buckled it on her hip. She grabbed her hat and jammed it on her head. Magic looked excited when he saw Sugar walk into the stable.

"Hello, Big Boy," she said feeling as happy to see him as he appeared to be to see her.

He stood still for her to slip his bridle into place and cinch up the saddle. She led him outside where she mounted and heeled him into a swift gallop toward town.

Sugar and Magic arrived on the outskirts of town

fifteen minutes faster than usual. Sugar pulled the stallion up to a trot when they reached the outskirts of town. She didn't't want to draw any attention. If anyone sees her, she can say she had to come to town to meet with Wayne Scott one of the Granbury Bank officer's about wiring Daddy some money for some supplies. She won't stay long. Just find out what Parker is up to and go home, she thought. She hoped it would be that simple.

She entered main street via a side street that placed her within the area Parker might feel the most comfortable. They had met at the Cattleman's Saloon. She could see the Granbury Bank down the street which would match with her reason for being in town. The Granbury Hotel stood across the street from the saloon. She could leave Magic at the bank and check out the hotel, then the saloon. The idea seemed reasonable considering she didn't't have a clue what she expected to find.

She rode Magic around to the back of the bank where he would be safe from covetous eyes. Mr. Scott, the head Cashier, agreed to watch out for him. Sugar walked to the hotel.

The lobby looked empty when she walked in. Lunch time, she thought. The register sat on the counter on a swivel. Sugar turned it around and read the names. Jim Parker, room 247, she turned the register back to its proper place. The keys hung on a large keyboard on the wall behind the desk. She walked around the desk and helped herself to the key.

The Granbury appeared to be a nice hotel with clean, fresh carpets, fresh paint and quality furnishings. Sugar stopped in front of door number 247 and gave it a firm knock. No one answered so she used the key and went in.

The room looked like any standard hotel room with a bed, a parlor area with a table and a washroom at the end of the hall. Sugar felt a momentary guilt for invading Parker's space but then she thought of him snooping through her house, going through her father's personal and private possessions without his knowledge or permission and the guilt turned into resentment.

Rachel and I were there, she thought. He could have asked, at least me if not Rachel, unless his snooping held an ulterior motive that he specifically did not want us to know about. Something about Daddy, she realized.

Determined now to find out the truth, she closed the door and crossed over to see what he had piled on the bed.

At first glance she thought the items looked like dirty old clothes he planned to throw away. But as she drew closer, she could see that Parker had divided the items into specific groups.

Sugar gently picked up the first item in the collection, a small piece of paper that appeared to be a folded over note.

"Jordan," she read aloud. "Meet me at midnight at the old livery shack. Q."

"What?" she whispered staring at the note in shock.

She reread the words several times before setting it back down where she had picked it up.

Her heart started beating a little faster and she felt herself breathing deeper.

Next, she picked up a crusty rope with cracklings of mud and some other dried rust colored substance flaking into her hands. She released the rope and it dropped onto the bed with a low "whomp." She dusted her hands on the bed cover.

Reluctant to touch the old clothes rolled into individual pieces, she covered her hand with the bed cover and unwound a shirt and vest also covered in the same dried mud and reddish flakes as the rope. They appeared large, the size her father might wear. She placed them back on the bed.

Then she noticed another larger note folded in half. For some reason, she felt reluctant to touch it. A thought she did not want to acknowledge began forming in her mind. She wanted to leave the door key on the table and run out of the room. She felt her heart beating faster now and her hands shook uncontrollably. She rubbed them together trying to steady herself.

Come on, Girl, you can't stop now, she urged.

Reaching down, she picked up the larger note. She opened it slowly and saw what she hoped she would not. There on the dirty paper she read the word, Sugar, her name written in blood. She set it back down quickly. That would certainly make Daddy furious, she thought.

And finally, she saw a smaller object wrapped in brown paper. Not wanting to touch it, she pinched hold of the corner of the paper wrap and let it unroll onto the bed. The knife shined up at her like some malevolent serpent ready to strike. She stepped away.

Looking around the room, she noticed some papers on the table. She walked over and picked them up. The top of the page read "Closing."

Underneath it read:

First degree murder must be proven by a preponderance of the evidence beyond a reasonable doubt.

Motive to Commit the Crime—Someone shot at daughter. Someone left a threat in the form of a slaughtered pig.

Means to Commit the Crime—Knife.

Opportunity to Commit the Crime—The night of the crime, father said he was going right to bed then left the house.

Sugar returned the papers to the desk almost in a trance. She couldn't believe her eyes as she took one last look around the room.

This is the proof Parker is going to use to convict my father of murder, she thought.

Then she corrected herself.

This is the stuff Parker is going to try to use to convict my father of murder, she thought. Hell will freeze over first, she swore.

The key clinked on the floor as she walked out.

Sugar kept Magic at a comfortable canter on the ride home. The more she tried to straighten out her thoughts, the more tangled they became. With Daddy out of touch, she would have to cope until he returned, she thought. One person she knew her father would trust, Sheriff Grady Speal, had stayed in Granbury to keep an eye out for any trouble in town. He would make an excellent ally. He and Quint had been friends for many years, worked together on community projects. He would stand up for her father.

CHAPTER 16

*Q*uint looked up into the unrelenting sun then wiped his face with his shirt front. Over one hundred men had made their way to Eagle Ford to build the Texas Pacific Railway track the rest of the final twenty-nine miles to Fort Worth. They started out in two shifts, one started at five in the morning ending at four in the afternoon. The second shift started at five in the afternoon until four in the morning. After three days of forming the soil to allow for drainage, setting the cross ties and rails and spiking each one in place, Quint and the other committee members realized they would never reach Fort Worth in two weeks. Completion would take more like two months. They scrapped the plan and started over.

They figured out that they could skip the soil work all together, lay the rail ties directly on the ground and instead of spiking the rails up one side and down the other, they could spike them once in the front on one side and once on the back on the other. Instead of taking time to build bridges over creeks, they simply suspended ties over the creek then placed the rails on the ties. That would hold for their purposes right now. Working on a new around the clock schedule, they would at least have a chance of finishing on time.

Two days before deadline, Quint figured, they were about four days away from the finish. In a desperate moment, Quint pulled Cody aside and told him to ride on into Fort Worth and tell the city council that if they want a railway, get out of bed and vote to move the city limit out two miles to meet the track. Cody rode as fast as his horse could go and returned the next day with a new city limit that put them one half mile inside Fort Worth. They kept the land grant and could send real railway workers to go back and "clean up" whatever needed "cleaning."

Loud shouts arose and hats flew into the air. They had met the timeline with a half day to spare!

Quint sent Cody to the nearest wire office to telegraph the town council in Granbury to plan a big celebration, "We did it and we're coming home tomorrow night."

Later that night, Quint stretched out in the roomy hauling wagon he bought to help move supplies along the construction line. Built in the fashion of a modified Conestoga, the first choice of most migrating pioneers, the wagon rode nicely over rough terrain and measured out as one of the largest domestic hauling wagons available. Quint looked forward to finding uses for it on the ranch. Sugar will want to order three or four more, he chuckled to himself. This was the first time he had thought about her since he left home two weeks ago. That's how much he trusted her to hold down the fort, he thought.

Now that the Jordan problem had resolved itself, sort of, Sugar will have an opportunity to pursue a path of her choice for her future. She has a good head on her shoulders. She'll find her way just fine, Quint thought. He felt excited to get home and settle back into his familiar old routine and not have the stresses of Sugar's ill-fated marriage. Even though the afternoon sun still hung high in the sky, he pulled the blanket he had brought from home over his head and drifted off to sleep the sleep of an exhausted and happy man.

Sugar swung down from Magic and secured him to the hitching post outside the Sheriff's office. She knocked and walked in. Grady sat at his desk drinking coffee and looked up.

"Hello, Sugar," he said looking into those gorgeous blue eyes and smiling as if pleased to see her. He had watched her grow from a pretty little girl to a beautiful young woman and like every other man that knew her, found her completely irresistible.

"What can I do for you today?"

"I need to talk to you about Daddy," she said, and her voice cracked. She cleared her throat. "Pardon me," she said trying to get control of her feelings. She would be of no use to her father if she broke down now, she thought. Calm down. Show confidence, she admonished herself.

She lifted her chin and took a breath and let it out slowly.

"Excuse me," she said. "I need to talk to you about Daddy," she said in a clear voice. "I need your help."

"What's going on?" he asked standing and pulling over a chair.

"Thank you." She sat on the edge of the chair.

He sat again behind his desk.

"Go ahead," he encouraged. "What can I do for you?"

"I heard a rumor in town that my daddy is under suspicion for the murder of Jordan Averill. Is that true?"

She watched his face for a reaction.

He looked down.

"Who have you talked to?" He looked back up at her and she took that as a bad sign.

"Just people. You know, somebody tells somebody and so on." She sounded flip to her own ears. She could only imagine what Grady thought. But she couldn't't say she broke into Parker's hotel room. Although, he may suspect she did if Parker already told him someone had.

She tried to look innocent.

"I can tell you this. Jim Parker was sent here to investigate the problem you and your father have with the Averills. He is good at his job and has done a thorough investigation. He is going over everything very carefully again and plans to announce his findings soon."

Sugar nodded her head.

"I am going to do everything in my power to help you and Quint, but you know the Averills are pressing hard for some kind of justice for their son. They have to be considered, too. That said, I am going to be there for you and your dad every step of the way so, don't you worry. It's going to be all right. Do you have any reason to think that it won't? Do you have any doubts about your father? Anything you want to tell me about?"

Sugar's body tensed with a combination of anger and fear, but she tried not to show it.

"No, of course not," she said smiling. "Everyone knows Daddy. Everyone knows he isn't capable of doing anything like that."

"I agree. Don't listen to gossip. Nobody knows what Parker is going to do. But whatever it is you and Quint have my support."

The sheriff stood and helped Sugar out of the chair.

As soon as she stood Grady wrapped his arms around her, pulled her against his chest and gave her a firm hug. She put her hands on his sides and gently nudged herself away. She didn't't like to be grabbed like that, but he was on her father's side. She looked up at him.

"Thank you so much, Sheriff. I appreciate your support." She smiled. "See you soon," she said turning toward the door.

He smiled and chuckled.

"Call me Grady," he said, "I'll see you soon."

He reached around her and opened the door.

"Thank you, Grady," she said and walked out. Magic snorted and dipped his head when he saw her coming.

"Yes, you're a good boy," she rubbed his soft muzzle then swung up onto his back and rode off toward home when she heard a man's voice call her name. She looked in his direction and saw Mr. Wheatly, the telegrapher waving a piece of paper at her. She pulled Magic to a stop.

"I have a telegram here says your father has finished the railroad and will be home tomorrow! There's going to be a big party!" He sounded excited.

Sugar felt both excited and relieved at the same time.

"That's wonderful news! Thank you, Mr. Wheatly!"

She heeled Magic into a gallop. Once out on the road, she gave Magic his head and held on for the ride.

"Rachel! Where are you?" Sugar yelled coming in the front door at home.

"In here," she yelled back as she came running from the kitchen. "What?" she said when she saw Sugar coming through the dining room.

"Great news! Daddy's coming home tomorrow," she said and stopped as tears of relief welled up in her eyes.

"That's good news," Rachel said with a puzzled look on her face.

"What is this? Tears?" She drew closer and Sugar started shaking.

"Aw now, Sweetheart. Why are you crying?" She gathered Sugar into her arms and gave her a motherly hug.

"Daddy's in terrible danger, Rachel, and we are going to have to help him. Who's in the house?"

Rachel stood back and waited for her to catch her breath.

"There's a girl, get control of yourself. Take your time," she said in a slow, soothing tone.

Sugar took a breath and let it out slowly as she had in the sheriff's office.

"Who is in the house?" she asked again sounding more in control.

"Just me, I think. And I saw Parker earlier in Quint's office."

Sugar took another breath and released it slowly.

"Thank you, Rachel," she said, "I need to talk to him. I'll find you later."

Rachel nodded her head and watched her walk into the study.

Outside, the sun had crawled behind a dark cloud throwing the study into a state of half shadows. Parker sat behind Quint's big wooden desk with his booted feet propped up on top of a stack of papers that had collected since Quint had left to save the railway. Parker's feet thumped to the floor and he sat upright when Sugar stopped in front of him.

She's so beautiful, he thought looking her up and down. He brought to mind the image of the afternoon she laid in his arms, naked, thrilling to his touch.

"I heard some disturbing talk today that I don't really believe but thought I would ask you about."

"What was that?" he said playing dumb.

"They said you were going to try to arrest my father for Jordan's murder." She felt her confidence growing now that she had spoken the words.

"Yes," he said unlike Grady, not equivocating at all. "Yes, because he did kill Jordan, and I have irrefutable physical evidence to prove it. You'll think so, too when you see it."

"I've already seen it," she said.

"I thought that was you," he said. "Don't worry. I know none of this was your fault. You don't have to feel guilty for wanting to be yourself. You wanted to be a good daughter. You were a young girl manipulated into an impossible situation. You love your father and have made him proud. But it's time for you to let him go and start your own life. You need to think about what direction you want your life to take. You need to get away from here and grow up."

He reached out to take her hand, but she stepped back.

"You've been spoiled, isolated, treated like a combination pet, daddy's girl, and princess of Granbury. Sometimes you still act like a child. All of your father's spoiling and isolating has stunted you emotionally. It's time to stand up and become a woman. Come away with me. We can have a good life together. There's more to life than protecting Daddy's money until the day you die."

"I'm not going to run away with you!" Sugar said. "I have obligations to the ranch my father and I built. People are depending on me to keep the bank running for them. I have a standing in Granbury. The people of this town need me to be here for them."

"That's where you're wrong," he told her. "That's your father talking through you."

"How totally arrogant and wrong you are! Don't tell me I'm wrong. You're wrong. My daddy is innocent, and I am going to prove it. You want me to go away with you? I have wasted four years of my life on a man already and look what happened. I'm only eighteen years old and I already know men are mean and a woman never knows what they are really thinking. No. I don't need anyone. Besides, I would rather live my life alone than be with the man who wants to murder my father."

Parker gritted his teeth until the muscles in his neck started to stand out. Her words stung him more than he thought they ever could.

"Lady, you have a lot of thinking to do before you can decide who really needs you or who you really need," he ground out through clenched teeth. I'm sorry but we have to be enemies for a while. I have a duty to do, but I'll be back. Think about what I've said. I'm serious about wanting you with me." He started toward her. She stepped back and held up her hands to hold him away. He turned and strode out of the house leaving her standing in the study, alone and afraid for her father.

She listened to the gathering storm outside as Parker left out the front door.

"Rachel," she called.

Rachel hurried into the study looking shaky herself.

"What's wrong? What's happened?"

"Something awful, something you won't believe."

Sugar took her by the hand and led her to the chair in front of Quint's desk. She sat in his big leather chair behind his desk and watched Rachel look around the room, wringing her hands. She looked down at the papers on the desk.

What would Daddy tell me to do? she wondered.

He would tell me to take care of business, she thought. She stiffened her spine and folded her shaking hands on top of the desk then took a breath and let it out slowly.

"Rachel, we have a problem."

Rachel nodded her head and kept listening.

"It seems that Jim Parker thinks he has figured out who killed Jordan."

Her eyes widened.

"Who?" she said.

"Daddy," Sugar said.

"Oh! No!" she stood up and walked behind her chair. "He is wrong! Your father would never do anything like that!"

"I know, but we are past that point, I'm afraid. Parker said he has enough evidence to prove in court he is guilty. I have seen the evidence, it looks bad. Parker has a story of how it happened and uses the evidence to back it up. I am going to have to prove that story wrong."

"How are you going to do that?" Rachel said walking back around the chair and sitting down.

I'm not sure yet, but I know Daddy is innocent, so I know there is a way. I just have to figure out what it is. In the meantime, things are going to get crazy around here. I am going to talk to Daddy. He is getting home sometime tomorrow afternoon. They saved the railway," she said as an afterthought.

"That's wonderful. I hope people will see what a good man he is and listen to you."

"Me, too," Sugar said but did not expect anything. "The Averill's seem to be out for blood. They have friends, too, that will support them. When the arrest becomes public, we are going to have to be ready."

"Anything I can do to help, please tell me."

"For now, if anyone wants to talk about this, we should say, 'Sheriff Speal is leading the investigation and we believe in his ability to make a fair and just decision on how to proceed.' Don't get into a discussion or debate with anyone. Look calm, be confident, everything will work out fine. I'm going to talk to Daddy about it tomorrow. He has no idea this is happening," Sugar rubbed her forehead as if to clear her thoughts. "I'll let you know if anything else happens."

Rachel looked shaken. But, in time, she'll calm down, I'm sure, she thought.

Sugar jotted a few notes about points she did not want to forget then made her way to her bedroom. Outside, the wind began to whip around and make a high-pitched screaming sound blowing through the wire garden fence.

Suddenly, Sugar's thin shell of confidence shattered

and whatever she had told herself to get through the day gave way. A choking fear welled up into her chest.

Thunder boomed and a sudden crack of lightening flashed in the window. Sugar looked just in time to see the outline of a man peering in at her. She ran to the wardrobe and grabbed her gun out of the holster but by the time she returned to the window the form had disappeared into the black pouring rain. She ran over to her side table and turned down the light then ran back, but he was gone. A sudden chill shivered through her. She walked back to her bed.

"Daddy," she called to her empty house, but no one was there to answer. Shaking uncontrollably, she slipped her gun under the pillows then crawled under the covers and pulled them over her head.

CHAPTER 17

Sugar's eyes popped open. She slowly scanned the room making sure she was alone, then carefully slid her six- shooter from its hiding place under the pillow. She jumped out of bed, softly stepped to the door and opened it enough to hear men's voices in the kitchen but she couldn't make out any words. Rachel's laugh carried across the hallway and Sugar let out a sigh of relief. Walking to the wardrobe where her gun belt dangled from a metal hook, she slid the pistol back into its holster.

She pulled on her work clothes and hurried to the kitchen to see who had come to visit this early.

"Cody!" she said in delight.

He smiled and stood just in time to catch her as she wrapped her arms around him in a welcoming hug.

"I am so glad to see you," she said.

"I see that," he said.

She laughed and tried to pull away, but he held her one more moment before letting her go.

Realizing she hadn't even looked at the others in the room, she smiled at Rachel then turned to see Grady Speal sitting and smiling at her, a cup of coffee on the table by his hand.

"Good morning, Sheriff."

Why was he here? she wondered as she reached forward and shook his hand.

"Good morning," he said.

"I'm sorry, don't let me interrupt your conversation," she said helping herself to a cup of coffee. She sat in a chair between Cody and Grady. "Go ahead," she said.

"I was just telling Sheriff Speal about the railway construction."

"Where is Daddy?" she asked.

"He'll be here soon," Cody said. "He is bringing back a wagon he bought in Dallas. It moves slower than I wanted to go. I rode ahead. Your father wants to have a celebration tonight in town. I thought I'd come in early to get that set up."

He looked at Grady.

"What do you think, Sheriff? Maybe speakers can stand in Quint's wagon and make some speeches then they can adjourn to the Cattleman saloon for free drinks?"

"That sounds fine and count me in," he said taking a quick glance at Sugar.

"Okay, I'll tell Quint."

Sugar stood with her coffee cup in hand.

"I want to finish my rounds before Daddy gets here." She looked down thinking about the news she had to tell him.

She walked out the back door.

Leaves and branches blown down by last night's storm

lay scattered around the backyard. Sugar took a pitchfork out of the barn and scraped the debris into a pile and left it for one of the hands to pick up and take to the burn area.

That's better, she said to herself, then stopped and slowly scanned the area again remembering the howling wind against the windows, the debris pounding against the house, the man shaped phantom in the window and the shivering cold that chased her under her heavy bedcovers to hide from the storm. She still felt the same fear right now. But the storm is over, she thought, swept away into a pile of scraps easily dealt with. A sudden insight occurred to her. Actually, it's the fear of the storm that lingers, not the storm itself, she realized. There's no sense in being afraid of a storm that is over. And there's no sense in being afraid of a storm that isn't here yet, she thought. Life is full of storms. Hide if you have to, then clean up and move on.

She headed for the stable to saddle Magic when she heard what sounded like a passing carnival. She watched as a group of about twenty men on horses riding alongside an oversized odd-shaped wagon painted bright blue with red wheels came lumbering up the approach to the ranch whooping and singing like a bunch of drunken cowboys.

"Daddy!" she screamed and started running toward them. Finally, she thought, and the most thankful feeling flowed through her body. He's here, he's here, she said over and over until she finally met up with him. He halted the four large draft horses pulling the wagon and reached down to grab her hand to help her up beside him.

He looked so glad to see her. She thought, at first, he

would never release her from his bear hug he always gave her when he had been away. She finally fought her way loose and everyone laughed and clapped and started telling their stories of their adventures of the past two weeks.

People nearby came running to see the happy heroes who had saved the railway. Sugar had not seen her father this happy ever. He looked thinner and as if he had not bathed since leaving two weeks ago, but he looked handsome and ten years younger. Sugar wanted him to have this time of joy, but she had to talk to him right now.

"Daddy," she said pulling on his arm for attention. "Daddy, listen to me," she shouted in his ear.

"What, Sugar?" He turned toward her and saw the expression on her face. "What is it, Sweetheart?"

"Take me home. We need to talk, now."

She sat on the lazy board, where Quint had sat to drive the horses, and waited for him to extricate himself from the merry makers. He sent the riders ahead and he came to sit beside Sugar.

"Okay, what do we need to talk about that is so important?" he said.

"I wanted to catch you before you came home because I didn't't want you to be caught unawares. It's about Jordan's murder case. Jim Parker has a suspect and he is going to arrest him soon."

"That's good news. Who is he after?"

"You." Sugar said.

"Me?" Quint looked incredulous.

"What makes him think I did it?"

"He has evidence. Bloody clothes, a note and a knife."

"What makes him think they're mine?"

"I don't know, Daddy. But he has it all worked out. I think he is going to arrest you as soon as you go into town tonight."

"That gives us a little time. I think I'll wire a lawyer I know in Fort Worth to come on down and stay with us for a while to sort this out. How do you know about all this?" Quint said.

"He has moved to a hotel room even though he still comes to the house. Rachel saw him snooping around, so I went to town to find out what he was up to. I saw the evidence laid out on the bed in his hotel room along with a story he had written how each piece of evidence proved you killed Jordan."

Quint looked shocked.

"I've got news for him. Nothing he has could prove I killed anybody because I didn't't do it!" he said.

Sugar hugged him tight.

"We told him that." Sugar said.

"I know you did, Sugar." He sat down and drove the bulky wagon on to the house in silence.

Sugar learned his traveling companions turned out to be the hands from the ranch and some others who had volunteered from Granbury.

Quint put Cody in charge of the revelers and hurried into the house. He didn't know how much time he had before Parker and Grady showed up to arrest him, but he figured it wouldn't be too long. He wrote out the telegram to the lawyer in Fort Worth and Sugar had Cody pick out someone trustworthy enough to take it to town to send. He washed up as best he could with a ranch full of visitors and put on the first freshly washed clothes that he had worn in two weeks. He packed a small bag with toiletries and clean shirts and set it on Sugar's bed then went out to join the guests.

Outside, the congenial gathering had deteriorated into a milling crowd. Rachel, quickly transitioning from panic to unhinged, ran up to him holding a tray filled with sliced bread and onion.

"I have no food to feed these people and I am certainly not passing out fifths of your good whisky to everyone. They are thirsty and hungry. I think it would be best if you told them to go home and meet back in town for the festival or whatever this is."

Quint laughed.

"Good idea. I'll take care of that."

He jumped up onto his new wagon.

"Friends! Friends!" The noise died down to a buzz.

"Let's all go home, get freshened up, and meet again around four o'clock outside of the Cattleman. We'll speak a few words and have a few drinks! What do you say?"

Everyone cheered, mounted up and headed out. The Double Bar W hands retired to the bunk house and order returned to the yard. Rachel forced Quint to follow her into the kitchen so she could cook him a supper which left two lone people sitting on the fence railing around the first corral.

Cody took a sideways glance at Sugar. Two weeks had been too long of a time for him to be away from her. Having trouble controlling the urge to pull her down to the ground and make long, slow love to her right there, he slipped off the fence and put his hands on either side of her waist to lift her down. She landed so closely in front of him, all he had to do was lean in and take possession of her soft waiting lips. So, he did. In spite of his determination not to, he pressed his lips to hers and lost what little control he had left. His carefully cultivated nonchalance melted, and raw desire took its place.

Sugar pressed back then felt herself responding with the ardor of a woman ready to counter anything he had in mind. His lips felt like they could set her body on fire with their kisses and she moaned with desire rubbing her ample breasts against his hard-muscled chest until she felt a longing deep within the cavern between her legs. Cody moaned a lusty sigh ready to finish this right here and now.

Somehow, he found the strength to push away and let go of her. She opened her beautiful blue eyes looking so lost in all consuming lust he almost pulled her back into his arms.

"Sugar, Sugar," he whispered in her ear and watched her eyes slowly clear until she regained control. She smiled and laughed in delight at the passion they had found.

"Wow!" she whispered looking into his gorgeous gold flecked hazel eyes then fell forward against his firm chest.

"Your heart is beating so hard," she said.

"I know." He laughed. "Are you trying to kill me? Cause if you are, it'll be a mighty nice way to go."

I wish we were at the cove, she thought.

"I apologize, Sugar. This is not how I wanted our first moment to go."

"Don't you dare ruin my first moment, Cody Edwards. It was perfect and I will never forget it," she pretended to scold him.

He chuckled.

"You're shameless, Miss Wildcat."

"Could be," she teased, and he almost grabbed her again. "We need to hurry if we're going to town."

"That's true," she said. I'll meet you there. I'm going to ride along with Daddy in his wagon. I might need you to help me get it home." She didn't't want to tell him why just yet.

"Oh. You're not riding Old Mudd Pie?"

"Do you really think I would name my horse Old Mudd Pie?" She pretended she felt insulted.

Cody shrugged his shoulders.

"All right. I can leave my horse in the livery overnight," he said.

"Thank you," she said, "for everything." She gave him a sheepish smile.

He released her hand and missed her already. I'm in deep manure here, he thought and hurried to the bunkhouse.

Sugar hurried to her room. Conflicting feelings vied for her attention. In amongst the havoc of the last few weeks, an exciting element had hatched into her life. Cody! She hadn't realized how strong her feelings for him had grown. It had happened so naturally she had not thought anything special about it, like it was meant to be.

What did Ginger say? she thought.

"When you are ready, take control of your own life and find your happiness. You pick your own man. Nobody can tell you who to love."

"But, how will I know when I find the one man that I want?" I had asked her.

"Oh Honey, you'll know," she had said.

And what did Rachel say? she thought.

"It's just like learning to swim. You jump into the

water and start paddling. And be careful you don't drown."

I wonder what my mother would have said? she thought then remembered.

The letter! She never read the letter!

Sugar ran over to the bureau and opened the bottom drawer. She reached under the clothes where she had left it and there it was, waiting. She pulled the envelope out and ran over to the bed. "Sugar," it said across the front. Careful not to rip it asunder, she prized the flap open and took out a folded paper. She opened it and there in front of her eyes, her mother's words, written in her own hand, lay upon the page.

Sugar looked at the neat script marveling at both the pristine condition of the paper and beauty of the penmanship.

She read the words slowly, savoring each one.

"Dear Little One,"

"I am thinking of you at home asleep in your bed. It is two in the morning and I don't know if I'll make it, but I'm going to try and get back to you. I am sending this letter to your father to give to you on your eighteenth birthday in case I don't. You are five years old now. I may not be able to tell you what I want you to know, so I am writing it down in hopes you will get it someday. I wish I was there to see you all grown up. I know your father will raise you right, to be a good girl, educated, well married. Your father and I discussed that. We both decided that an arranged marriage would be best. We wanted to be sure you were set up in life and would never have

to struggle like we did. I hope he followed through with that. I'll tell you some about your father and me. We met in New Orleans in a pleasure house owned by my uncle. I was put to work at fourteen years old cleaning, cooking, running errands, helping the ladies dress, that kind of thing. I was not to be one of the fancy ladies. My momma and daddy forbad it. But the money was good, and the gentlemen liked me, so I started learning the trade behind their backs. At first, I had fun. There was a party every night. We drank champagne. Uncle made sure I didn't have any gentlemen I could not handle at fourteen years old. Then I turned fifteen and everything changed. Uncle sold out to a gambler who turned the house into a gambling den. All kinds of shenanigans started. We cheated, we stole, and worse. Thank God your father came in one night and talked to me. He thought I should not be there. He said I was too young. This was not good. He wanted to help me. He bought me from the gambler. He paid a large amount of money for me. The gambler told me to go with your father then runaway and come back to him. I agreed but I did not want to come back. I did not want to be a fancy lady anymore. So, I didn't run away. I stayed with Quint. When I turned eighteen, your father bought me a beautiful wedding dress and trousseau so we could marry. We married. I had you. We were happy. Then the gambler came to town. He recognized me. He said I had to go with him. I said no. He took me to his hotel room and tied me up. He bought me a horse. He made me write a letter to Quint saying I was leaving to go back with my gambler man and be a fancy lady. I don't know what happened to your father or you after that. The gambler man took me back to New Orleans and said he would kill me and my family if I ever ran away again. I did not. I was afraid for you and Quint. I had to protect you. I did not run away. But I realize *now that not seeing you is worse than death. I am leaving tonight. I hid some money from my earnings. I'm going to try to get back to you. If I don't make it, you must live a happy life in love and contentment for me as well as yourself. This is my only revenge. I want you to know this. Your father is a good man. He will give you all his love. He wants the best for you. He gave his best to me. Marry a good man like him and be happy. Don't marry a handsome gambler man. They are no good. You must remember, if you are looking for the right man for you, you mustn't only look with your eyes. You will not see him. You must learn to look with your heart as well. Then you will know it is him. You will just know. Like I did. I love you my precious Sugar. I hope to see you soon."*

"Mother"

A TEAR LANDED beneath the signature.

"Mother." Sugar said the name aloud. She ran her fingers over the words then hugged the paper against the strong beat of her heart. She finally knew the truth. She had a mother and she loved her, stood ready to die to see her again. She smelled the paper to try to pick up a scent from her. It smelled like moldy old paper. But she wanted Sugar to know her. She wanted to know me, she thought. She must have died trying. The knowledge weighed heavy on her mind.

Now I know what my mother would have told me about finding the right man.

"DON'T MARRY a handsome gambling man. They are no good. You must remember, if you are looking for the right man for you, you mustn't only look with your eyes. You will not see him. You must learn to look with your heart as well. Then you will know it is him. You will just know."

"Thank you, Mother," she said to the letter carefully folding it and replacing it into the envelope.

Sugar knew now that Nicolette loved Quint and herself. She wanted to be with them so badly that she used her love for them to defy the fear of death in order to get back home. She fought like a true hero, she thought. A growing respect for her mother filled the emptiness she had been feeling with a love and strength to stand on her own two feet, like her mother had done.

She heard a soft knock at her bedroom door.

"Time to go. Rachel and I will be waiting in the wagon," her daddy said.

Her heart swelled with a new love and understanding for him. She ran and hid the letter back where she had gotten it from her drawer.

"Be right there," she said and quickly finished dressing, grabbed her gun belt and the case her father had left on the bed and ran out to meet them.

CHAPTER 18

Even though in the midst of a crowd, he had to fight the compulsion to walk over to her window and look in. He hated seeing her in a crowd. He hated seeing all the men taking secret looks at her, fantasizing about her in their beds and what they would do with her there. They were disgusting. Especially when they all knew she was his.

He wished he could tell them she only loved him, but if he did, her father might find out and lock her away from him. My way would be better. I can take her far away where no one could find her. She won't be bothered by all these men who want to take her away from me. She'll be much happier.

He still had that sleeping potion he bought from the traveling medicine man in Fort Worth. He had his black clothes and black mask so he can maneuver invisibly in the dark.

He almost had everything together. He still had to build the box. But he needed to know her exact height and proportions to do that. He imagined her naked lying in wait for him in her secure box where no one else could touch her but him. The thought gave him an erogenous shiver. It wouldn't be long now. He rubbed his mouth with the back of his hand and smiled.

CHAPTER 19

Quint climbed up into the wagon and sat on the makeshift bench. Rachel had joined him and finally, Sugar ran out of the house carrying his case, her hairbrush, her gun belt with gun and a book titled, *Breeding the Perfect Arabian*. She threw her armload of must haves into the wagon and climbed up. Cody and Joseph and Buck rode alongside on their horses.

Quint shouted at the horses to git and they rolled out of the yard and onto the approach to the ranch. Sugar didn't't care what her father said about the easy ride, the wagon bucked and rolled and bounced until she felt sure her neck would break. But Quint looked happy, so she didn't't complain. They bumped along the road to town finally arriving with five minutes to spare. Sugar commented the ride took forever, but Quint argued it had only been half that long. Sugar informed him that half of forever is still a long, long time. He agreed with that.

The railway workers, in order to get to the real reason for coming tonight, free drinks, spoke their piece quickly and succinctly about how so many people with a noble common purpose could accomplish the impossible if they applied themselves. The good people of Granbury should feel a sense of pride in their fellow citizens for their self-lessness and sacrifice to make Granbury the greatest town in Texas.

Finally, to everyone's delight, Cody stepped up to the speech area to make the last speech.

"All what we have said here tonight is true, except the part about Buck working so hard. I mostly saw him sleeping on the flour sacks waiting for dinner. Everyone laughed and Buck pretended to hide behind his hat in embarrassment. But the boys and I wanted to say a special 'Thank you' to the man who had a vision to make things better around here and saw it through to a successful end, the man who made this whole project a reality, Mr. Quinton Wylie!"

Sugar watched everyone whoop and throw their hats and pat Quint on the back and generally show an honest respect to this amazing man. She felt an over whelming pride as Quint stepped up and looked at each person standing around him.

"I love every one of you," he said in a gravelly voice, "Let's go get drunk!" he yelled.

Everyone laughed and headed over to the Cattleman Saloon. Then she spotted them. Jim Parker and Sheriff Grady Speal walked up to the father she adored. Fear, dark and vivid, gripped her.

Parker spoke.

"Quint Wylie, you are under arrest for the murder of Jordan Averill."

He took out a pair of handcuffs and clicked them

around Quint's wrists. Sugar watched as all of her protective instincts kicked in.

"Go on and wait at the Cattleman," Parker commanded. "I'll come get you when he can have a visitor."

"Thank you, but I think I'll sit right here," she said sitting in the wooden chair the Sheriff sometimes sat in during the day. Cody pulled over a chair and joined her.

Parker looked like he wanted to argue with her, then thought better of it.

"Okay," he said and took Quint inside and shut the door.

Cody looked worried.

"You knew about this, didn't't you?"

"I knew what Parker was up to, but I didn't't know for sure they were going to act tonight," she said. "I thought we had more time."

"Did you get to talk to your father about what to do?"

"Yes. That telegram I asked you to have sent went to an attorney in Fort Worth that Daddy knows. He is supposed to come tomorrow. I can't see them setting bail, but the trial should start in a few days."

"Parker has some evidence he thinks tells how Daddy committed the murder, but Daddy said he didn't't commit the murder, so Parker couldn't't prove anything."

Cody understood her concern, but she could do little here except get herself hurt if trouble arose.

"Why don't you get somebody to take you home. I'll stay with him all night," he said.

"I'm not going anywhere," Sugar said scrunching down in her seat as if gluing her pants to the chair. "I would appreciate you staying with me, though."

"Of course, I'll stay with you," he said putting his arm around her. He leaned over and gave her a light kiss.

She smiled her appreciation and sat back, because whatever happened from then on, she planned to call this chair home until she walked beside her father out of that jail. She stretched her legs out and crossed them at the ankles then lowered her hat over her eyes.

In what seemed like a minute, Sugar's eyes jerked open and she straightened herself in the chair. An incessant rustling noise like horses stomping impatiently thrummed in her ears.

I must have fallen asleep, she thought, trying to wipe the grit out of her eyes so she could see. She looked around and thought she saw someone across the street looking at her, but she couldn't't make out who it was. She blinked and squinted. Finally, her vision cleared, and she saw only an empty street. She stared around in confusion then remembered. Parker and Grady had arrested Daddy and they told her to wait here.

How long ago was that? she wondered. She stood and looked through the window of the jail house. She didn't see anyone, so she tried the door. It creaked opened. She walked inside the log building then stopped and looked around. She stood in a room with a desk and chair and a cot on the other side. A closed door with a ring of keys and two racks of rifles wrapped in chain and secured with a large metal lock hung on the wall beside it.

Sugar walked over to the door and opened it to see two rows of cells, all but one empty. She hurried over and looked in. Her father lay sleeping on the bare cot fully dressed and snoring the snore of an exhausted sleeper.

"Daddy," she said. "Daddy," she said louder. "Daddy," she yelled.

Quint flinched and raised his hands as if ready for someone to deliver a blow.

Sugar ran out and grabbed the ring of keys off the wall and ran back inside to her father's cell. She kept sticking keys in the lock until one clicked it open. Only one dim light burned in the front room. Quint could not see who had come into the cell. He still wore the handcuffs.

"Daddy, are you all right?" Sugar said.

"Sugar! Find the keys to these will you?" he held up the cuffs.

She ran to the other room, looked around, then went over to the desk and opened the drawer. She found a smaller set of keys, grabbed the lamp, and returned to her father.

"Are you alone?" Quint said.

"No. Cody was with me. I guess he left. I fell asleep. We have been waiting for Parker or Grady to let us in to see you. I don't know where they are, either."

"They probably didn't't go far," he said. "Let's sit and wait for them to come back."

"Okay."

Sugar walked over to the door to close it and a group of about five people wearing white hoods and carrying burning torches sat on horses and glared down at her through what looked to her like empty black eyeholes. The lead rider held a coiled rope and swung it in the air.

"Quint Wylie! Come out and face your vengeance!" he said in a low sing-song voice.

"Arthur Averill, is that you?" Sugar said.

Inside, Quint had opened the rifle cabinet and taken

out several loaded rifles ready to fire. He cocked the double-barreled shotgun he had picked out and shot the first barrel into the roof of the jailhouse. Outside, the horses' eyes bulged, and they began to shy and prance. He started to shoot the other barrel, then heard a pistol shot and felt it hit his shoulder. He clutched the wound and fell to the floor. Sugar ran to him. He needs a doctor, she thought cocking the Henry repeater she held. She stood, whirled around and took aim at the first sheet head she saw.

"Bam!" the rifle exploded, and a shot flew right over Arthur's head. "Bam!" another flew over the rider next to him.

"Let's get out of here," someone said.

"Wait," she heard Arthur say, but white sheets billowed as the riders took off as fast as they could go down the road and out of town.

Cody ran up in time to see them leave.

"What happened?" he said. He looked around for Grady, but he didn't't see him. He was just here, he thought.

"Daddy's been shot. He needs a doctor," Sugar said breathing in large gulps of air.

"Here," Cody said. "You sit here and help your dad. I'll go get the doctor."

Sugar looked up at him.

"Be careful," she said.

He ran off in the direction of the saloon.

Sugar could see the blood gushing out around her father's hand. Quickly she tore off her shirt sleeve and tied it around him as tightly as she could a couple of inches above the wound. She turned up a wooden chair and smashed the rungs with her booted foot. She took one of the rungs and slid it under the tied shirt and twisted as far as her strength allowed.

The bleeding slowed significantly so she tucked the rung in place and tried to get her dad up off the floor.

"Come on, Dad, try. Come on,"

She pulled and cajoled until she finally helped him onto the closest cot. He rolled onto his back and passed out.

Cody ran in with the doctor. "I'm going to get his bag," Cody said and ran back out and down the street.

"He's bleeding bad," Sugar told the doctor.

Doctor Harlin Daniels kept his eyes on his patient and spoke in a soft, calm voice. "Someone made a nice tourniquet. Was that you?"

"Yes," Sugar said looking at the blood soaking into her camisole.

"Very good job," he told her, "now you go over there and calm down. I've got this. Don't worry."

She did what he said.

As soon as Cody returned with the bag and handed it to the doctor, he sat down by Sugar. "Come here." He removed his shirt and wrapped it around her then laid her head in his lap.

"You okay?" he said.

"I am now,," she said.

The doctor got Quint's bleeding under control and Cody helped the patient to his feet.

"Can you walk?" the doctor said.

"Yes," Quint said.

"Come with me," the doctor said to Cody

and Sugar. "Let's go down to my office. I need to get

this as clean as possible," he said helping them down the street.

"What about the Sheriff? I'm arrested," Quint said.

"Well, you can be arrested at my place," the doctor said, and they kept walking.

Grady stepped out of the Cattleman Saloon and walked in the direction of the jail. A small crowd had gathered outside.

Quint supporters, he thought, but as he drew closer, he spotted the door swinging open. He hurried over pushed through the people and looked inside to see rifles torn off the wall, furniture shattered and splinters falling from the ceiling. The door to the lock up stood wide open. He walked inside to find Quint's cell empty.

He returned to the front office to take a closer look when he spotted the blood on the floor and cot. He found the keys, locked up and headed for the doctor's office.

The sheriff opened the door of the doctor's office and walked in.

"What's going on here?" he demanded.

Cody, Sugar, Doctor Daniels, and Quint all turned to look at him.

"Hello, Sheriff. Have a seat. I have your prisoner here safe in my custody," Doctor Daniels said and turned back to cleaning Quint's wound.

Sugar walked over to sit beside Grady.

"We had a problem," Sugar said. "Arthur Averill and some friends decided to save the judge the trouble of having a trial."

"Arthur?" Grady sounded taken aback as if that couldn't't possibly be true.

"Yes," Sugar said. "I recognized his voice."

"What do you mean?"

"There were about five or six of them all with white hoods over their heads."

Grady scratched his chin.

"But you didn't't see any of them?"

"No. But I did hear Arthur. He said, 'Quint Wylie. Come out and face your vengeance.'"

Quint nodded his head.

"That's what he said."

Cody looked at the Sheriff.

"Why don't you ride out and see what he is doing now?"

"I don't know," Grady said. "I better wait to get Quint locked up first. I'll have to find Parker to guard him."

"He's at the Cattleman's," Cody said.

"Okay. Let me work this out. I'll be back, Doc," he said and walked out of the door.

Word spread quickly about the failed lynching at the Cattleman's Saloon. Free whisky had poured all evening. The pros and cons of lynching grew louder and louder until factions formed with shouts calling for action to prove the point taking a serious turn. Grady decided to let things calm down until morning, besides he couldn't't find Parker.

Everything would look better in the morning, he decided and bedded down for the night.

THE MORNING BROUGHT good news for Sugar and her father. Quint's old friend and attorney, Robert Jakes, arrived on the first run of the Fort Worth to Granbury stage the very next morning. Not wanting to waste any time, Jakes had his bags taken to the Granbury Hotel and went straight to the jail to find Quint. He introduced himself to Grady and explained why he had come. Grady explained the happenings of last night and directed him to Doctor Daniel's office.

Quint and Sugar sat at the doctor's table eating a light breakfast of biscuits and cheese grits when the lawyer entered.

Quint stood and shook the other man's hand. Standing next to Quint, Robert Jakes looked like a small statured man, with dark curly hair, intelligent brown eyes and a mustache styled in the latest fashion. Judging from the expensive looking suit and obviously professional grooming, he looked every bit of a successful lawyer.

"Robert," Quint said in his big voice. "Thank you for coming." Quint looked happy to see him and more than a little relieved.

"May I present my daughter, Sugar? Sugar this is my friend Mr. Jakes."

"Nice to meet you, Mr. Jakes."

"Please, call me Robert, Miss Sugar." He smiled showing straight white teeth.

She smiled and nodded.

Won't you join us? Quint said. Robert sat and Quint handed him a plate.

"Cheese grits, Robert?" Sugar held up a serving.

"Yes. Please. I haven't had grits in years. I've always loved them since I was a young boy."

Sugar liked Robert immediately. She felt she had known him for years instead of minutes. She suspected most people felt the same. That pleasing personality probably had much to do with his success as an attorney, she thought.

"So, Quint, give me a run-down on what we're looking at."

Quint looked serious and said, "Murder."

Robert stopped eating and looked at him.

"Okay. Start from the beginning. Don't leave anything out."

Quint put his fork down and started at the beginning, not stopping until the very end.

Robert blinked and scratched his ear.

"Do you have any witnesses to corroborate your side of the story?"

"I do have my housekeeper who cleaned my drawers the morning Parker claims to have found the knife there. She will swear there was no knife in that drawer an hour earlier. I had been out of town building the railway at that time. So, I couldn't't have put it there after she finished. No. I didn't't hurt Jordan. I didn't't even call him out on taking a shot at Sugar. I was plenty mad, but I went to Grady for help instead of taking things into my own hands. Sheriff Speal will swear to that."

"What about the bloody clothes?" he said.

"I don't know what clothes he's talking about. I haven't seen those clothes and I don't know where he got them."

"Okay," Robert said. "I am scheduled to meet the judge this morning. I'm going over to the hotel to freshen up. I will make an appeal to have the trial scheduled for as soon as possible because of the lynching attempt last night. I'm going to try for one day this week. Are you up for that?"

"Yes, the sooner the better."

"Okay. We have a plan. I'll come see you after I talk to the judge."

Quint shook Robert's hand again.

"Thank you, Robert. I owe you a big one."

"Glad I can help." He said and left.

"I've been thinking, why don't you get a room at the Granbury?" Quint looked at his daughter. Her eyes looked slightly swollen and her hair could use a wash. She looked tired. "If you are going to stay with me, you'll have a place to freshen up, take a nap, do girl things. Go shopping. You need some pretty dresses."

Sugar smiled at her Daddy. Mother was right, she thought. He is a good man. He didn't't deserve all this trouble. But how can I prove it in court?

CHAPTER 20

*S*ugar took her father's advice and booked a room at the Granbury Hotel. The bowl of warm water proved sufficient for a body refresh and hair wash. The bed provided a place for a nice nap leaving Sugar ready for the night ahead watching over her father. The hotel stood between Doctor Daniel's office and the jail, a convenient location even taking into account she had to pass the Cattleman Saloon each way.

Quint seemed to take everything in stride. Grady agreed to allow Quint to stay with the Doctor as long as needed. Cody had arranged meals delivered to Quint from the hotel dining room. Sugar had her room close by. And his attorney arrived to hit the ground running on his defense. Even in crisis her dad knew how to take command.

"All we have left is the trial," Sugar thought as she entered Dr. Daniels' office to see Robert Jakes sitting and talking to her dad right now.

Quint looked up and smiled.

"Hi, Sweetheart. Everything okay with the hotel room?"

"Very comfortable," she said smiling. "Hello, Robert."

"Hello, I was just telling your father about the trial options."

"Okay. Please continue."

He turned his attention back on Quint.

"We can go ahead in two days with the judge only, or we can wait a week for the court to assemble a jury and that could lead to other difficulties. Like I said, the Averills are demanding a change of venue because of your notability in the area. They are convinced no unbiased juror exists within all of Hood County."

Quint knew which he would choose for himself, but would that choice be the best for the outcome of his trial?

"What do you think, Rob?"

"If I were you, I would forego the jury and trust in Judge Goins. He is a fair man and usually uses the law as the measuring stick for guilt or innocence. I have found in my practice that when people start manipulating juries, outcomes become sketchy. If I am going to have a jury, I want to know as much as possible where they might stand from the beginning. Some jurists go on gut feelings, some go on letter of the law as they understand it which may or may not be correct. Some do listen and make fair decisions. Best case scenario, I would go with the judge, but this is your trial."

"I think you're right. Let's get this over with. Two days? Sugar? Is that okay with you?"

"Sure," she said.

"Good," Robert said. "I would like to go over some

things with you and Sugar today and tomorrow. The trial will start Friday morning at nine a.m. Okay?"

"Sounds good." Quint rubbed his hands together like someone preparing for a good fight.

Two days later, Jim Parker, Chief Investigator and Acting Prosecutor, sat in the prosecutor's chair at the Hood County Courthouse and presented his evidence in his mind one more time. He had planned on having a jury to persuade. He had not prepared for a judge to reach the final decision. He hoped his analysis of the evidence stood up to the law as much as it did to common sense. Anyone who listened to him would conclude that common sense showed Quint killed Jordan. But judges liked to poke holes in conclusions. He hoped this judge wasn't one of them.

Sugar walked into the courtroom wearing a demure pale amethyst walking dress with a rounded neckline and a waterfall of flounces in the back instead of a bustle. She had twisted her beautiful onyx hair into a conservative bun low on the back of her head and plain black walking shoes on her feet. She looked like the wealthy young woman she was.

Quint wore a well-fitting blue suit that fit a touch tighter over his bandaged shoulder, not too formal, not too casual. He, too, looked like a man of his station, without pretense or rancor.

Both Sugar and Quint had dressed as Robert had instructed.

Robert wore a three-piece navy-blue suit making him look more like a professor in a university than a successful attorney.

Robert waited at the defense table for Quint.

Grady escorted him into the room then unlocked the handcuffs and sat in the chair behind him.

Observers crowded in until they filled all the gallery seats. Court officials closed the doors, and everyone stood for the judge. Judge Roy Goins entered, took his seat at the official bench and banged his gavel on the wooden trivet.

"This court will come to order for case number 30668, State of Texas versus Quint Wylie, Murder in the First Degree."

He banged his gavel again.

"Mr. Parker, are you prepared?"

Parker stood.

"Yes, Your Honor."

"Mr. Jakes, are you prepared?"

"Yes, Your Honor."

"Mr. Parker, you may deliver your opening arguments."

"Thank you, Your Honor."

Parker stood and lifted a leather case from under the table. The people in the gallery watched with curiosity while he took out each piece of evidence he had found and displayed it on the table in front of him.

He turned sweeping his hand over the items and addressed the gallery.

"As you know, first degree murder must be proven guilty by a preponderance of the evidence beyond a reasonable doubt. My plan is to present the irrefutable evidence that will prove guilty by a preponderance of this evidence beyond a reasonable doubt. To prove guilt, I will meet the requirements by showing the Three Indicators of Suspicion."

"Did the accused have a motive to commit this crime? Yes, after the victim fought with Wylie's daughter, someone shot at her only missing because she moved, and the bullet barely flew over her head."

"Did the accused have the means to commit this crime? Yes, he hid the knife used to take Jordan's life in his bedroom bureau where I found it."

Did the accused have the opportunity to commit the crime? Yes, on the night of the crime, the defendant told me he was going to bed, then minutes later I heard a horse riding away.

And finally, I will provide you a timeline showing how the accused sent the victim a note to meet him at the livery shack, waited in the dark for the victim to come in, then leapt upon him and slashed him in the neck until he was dead. He left the victim in the seldom used shed possibly never to be discovered."

"Thank you, Your Honor."

Thank you, Mr. Parker."

"Mr. Daniels."

"Thank you, sir."

Robert stood and slowly strolled back and forth across the room in front of the Judge as he talked.

"Mr. Parker speaks the truth when he says he found some key evidence in this case. And he did a fine job of investigating. But he goes awry in his interpretation of the evidence. Without any witnesses to corroborate, he wandered into the realm of conjecture. Although his conjecture sounds plausible, plausible is not the same as beyond a reasonable doubt. I will show the implausibility of the conjecture and bring in witnesses to cast light on some of the assertions."

"Thank you, Your Honor."

Robert sat down.

Quint and Sugar sat like statues in their chairs as Robert had instructed.

"Your floor, Mr. Parker." The Judge said.

"Yes, Thank you, Your Honor."

Parker stood and picked up a small piece of paper from the table.

"Jordan, meet me at the old livery shack at midnight. Q."

"This note came out of the victim's pocket while he waited at the Funeral Parlor to be prepped for burial."

Constance Averill began to cry.

"The Judge tapped his gavel on the trivet.

"Quiet, Please."

Constance covered her mouth with her handkerchief.

"Only in the most amazing coincidence ever would a father have sent a note with the name that begins with a 'Q' to a son-in-law who wants to kill his daughter. And the note is in the dead son-in-law's pocket, would he?" he said, his voice dripping with sarcasm.

"A slaughtered pig nailed to the back porch with his daughter's name stuck to it with a knife surely couldn't't make the father mad and prod him into doing something rash, could it?" he quipped.

"The father didn't't keep the knife as a memento to celebrate his daughter's freedom from a psychotic son-in-law, did he?" More sarcasm.

"Not unless his name is Quint Wylie. He would. He could. And he did," Parker said in disgust.

"The evidence clearly shows that Quint Wylie, saddled with a son in law, Jordan Averill, who had been forced into a marriage with an underaged girl grew disgruntled and took his frustration out on the girl trying to scare her off with dirty tricks. The defendant took the law into his own hands and got rid of the problem. Now he has to pay the price."

I rest my case."

Parker sat back in his chair.

"Thank you, Mr. Parker," The Judge said.

"Mr. Jakes."

"Thank you, Your Honor."

Robert stood and walked over to the Prosecutor's Table and picked up all of the evidence and carried it to the defense table. He spread it out so he could see it. He lined up the bloody clothes so Quint could make a thorough inspection of them. Robert selected the note first.

"I request for Mr. Wylie to be sworn in," he said.

The Court Clerk swore him in.

"Mr. Wylie, is this your handwriting?"

"No, Sir. It is not."

Robert handed him a pen and small piece of paper.

"Will you please copy this note for the court."

"I will be happy to," Quint said. He wrote the note in his normal handwriting. He handed the finished copy to Robert.

"Would you please look at these clothes," Robert said.

Quint picked up the pants, then shirt and held them up to his body then set them down.

"I don't recognize these clothes but I'm not absolutely sure. I don't really pay that much attention to clothes," he said honestly. "These are mighty dirty."

"What about this knife?" Robert said.

"I know I've never seen that knife."

"How did it get in your sock drawer?" Robert asked.

"I don't know," Quint said.

"On the night of the murder, where did you go after you told Mr. Parker you were going to bed?"

"I went to bed. I didn't't go anywhere."

"Did you hear any sounds of someone riding away when you went to bed."

"Not that I recall." Quint said.

"Mr. Wylie, did you murder Jordan Averill?"

Quint held fast to his control.

"No, I did not!" he said and looked at Arthur Averill.

Arthur looked down.

"That's all, Mr. Wylie. The defense calls Mrs. Rachel Strom, please."

Rachel looked pretty in a pink walking dress with a squared neckline and no bustle. She had twisted her dark gray hair into a knot on top of her head. She sat in a chair in front of the room. The Court Clerk swore her in.

Robert walked up to her and smiled a reassuring smile.

"Mrs. Strom, do you remember when you cleaned Mr. Wylie's bureau drawers last?"

"Yes, I do," Rachel said.

"When was that?"

"It was the same day Mr. Quint left for Fort Worth to save the train," she said. "I remember exactly because I knew he would be away for two weeks and I thought I would give his whole room a good cleaning. I went ahead and cleaned the drawers and folded the clothes in them. I threw away the worn socks and turned the mattress which is hard to do. Then about an hour later, I walked by the room and the drawers stood open and socks were all over the floor and the mattress was crooked."

"What did you do?" Robert asked.

"I straightened it out again."

"And during the times you were going through Mr. Wylie's drawers, did you see a knife like this one anywhere?"

He held up the knife.

"No, Sir. There wasn't any knife like that or any other knife in Mr. Quint's room."

"Thank you, Mrs. Strom," Robert said and helped her out of the chair.

"And finally, Your Honor, I would like to call Mrs. Sugar Averill to the front of the room."

Robert had warned Sugar in advance that the Judge would refer to her as Mrs. Averill. She had practiced not flinching in front of the mirror as Robert had suggested, but she felt guilty when the judge said the name in court. She had never been Mrs. Averill in her mind. She felt dishonest pretending to do so now.

"Mrs. Averill," the Judge said. Sugar walked to the chair and sat down.

The Court Clerk swore her in.

"Hello, Mrs. Averill."

"Hello," she said and smiled.

Robert picked up the copied note that Parker had taken from Jordan's vest and handed it to her.

"Would you please read this note and tell me if that is your Father's handwriting."

'She read the note and said, "Yes, this is my father's handwriting." A sudden gasp arose from the crowd.

She picked up the other note. "

"This is not my father's handwriting," she said and handed him the original note.

"Thank you," Robert said taking the two notes. "Please mark this note A and this note B," Robert said handing the notes to the Clerk. A says Jordan on the back and B says Wylie. Thank you," he said to the clerk.

"Please look at these clothes, Mrs. Averill. Do they look familiar? Have you seen your father wearing these clothes ever?"

Sugar looked at the clothes on the table, then at the boots.

"These are my boots," she said. Robert looked at the Judge. The Judge sat up straight and peered over the desk at Sugar.

"What makes you think those are your boots?" he said.

"Because these are my most comfortable boots. I wear them for work. I've been looking for these," she said and picked them up as if to take them home.

"Will you try those on for me," the Judge said.

"Yes, Sir." She hiked her skirt to mid calf and slid each soft leather, custom made boot on one foot at a time and up almost to each knee. She stood and walked around gracefully, as if she were wearing comfortable slippers.

Everyone in the room stared in confusion. Those were the clothes Quint supposedly wore to kill Jordan. They had dried blood smeared all over them. Sugar felt so happy to find her boots, she didn't't see the shock on Parker's face.

She heard the Judge say, "Mrs. Averill, will you please take off those boots and hand them to your father?"

"Yes, Sir." She did what he said.

"Mr. Wylie, will you please put those boots on?"

Quint looked at the Judge then at Robert. Robert nodded.

Quint put one boot on the end of his toes and pulled as hard as he could, but no way was that size eight boot going onto that size fourteen foot. He looked up at the judge and shrugged.

"This is my daughter's boot," he said. "I can't wear it."

"Will Mr. Parker, Mr. Jakes, Mr. Wylie, Mrs. Averill, and Mrs. Strom please join me in my Chambers. The rest of you, take a twenty-minute recess." He hit the gavel on the desk and tossed it down.

The Judge's Chambers were not built to hold six people, but six people crowded into the room just the same. Judge Goins stepped out to remove his robe then returned and sat behind a mahogany desk.

"All right, let's clear this up. He looked at Parker. You are asking me to convict a man of first-degree murder based on this evidence?"

"Yes, Sir," Parker said.

"Do you have any witnesses or experts to back up your deductions regarding this evidence?"

"No, Sir."

"I see."

"Mr. Jakes, would you like to make a motion right now?"

"Yes, Sir," he said.

"Let's adjourn to the courtroom." Goins shooed everyone out.

Back in the courtroom Judge Goins called for order.

"Mr. Jakes, you have the floor."

Robert Jakes rose from his seat at the defense table, straightened his coat and stood at attention.

"Your Honor," he said in a clear voice, "I move for a dismissal of this case with a finding in favor of the

Defense of Innocent Due to Lack of Evidence with immediate release of the prisoner."

"Granted," the Judge said and slammed down his gavel.

Sugar jumped up and ran over to her father and hugged him until he couldn't't breathe.

Robert walked over and shook hands with everyone.

"Congratulations," he said to Quint.

"Congratulations to you!" Quint patted him on the shoulder. "You are a life-saver and I'm not kidding."

They all laughed.

"I need to take care of some paperwork here, then I'll come find you. Where will you be?"

"The dining room at the Granbury Hotel," Sugar said.

"Perfect!" he said and watched the happy group hug all the way out the door. They found Cody sitting outside the courthouse with a rifle across his lap. He stood when he saw them.

"We won!" Sugar said, her blue eyes twinkling with happiness and excitement. "What are you doing out here?"

"Just waiting." He nodded at Quint and cleared the unspent bullet from the chamber. "Where to now?"

Sugar curled her free arm around his, pulled him into their group and they proceeded on their merry way.

FINALLY, back in her own bedroom, Sugar held her mother's letter gently in her hand. The small celebration at the Granbury had been light-hearted with good food, potent drinks and blessed relief from the stress of the weeks' events. Sugar and Quint couldn't't stop thanking Robert for coming so quickly to their aide and doing such a professional job. By the end of the party, everyone who had gathered to support Quint had decided Robert Jakes was hands down the best attorney in the world. When the time came for him to leave, the group carried his luggage to the stagecoach, gave hearty waves all around and sang his praises until the stage drove out of sight.

With the trial over, Sugar felt the weight from the fear for her father lift from her mind and body. But she knew the Averills still felt justice had not been served and they were only taking a breather to regroup for the next attack.

She and Quint both must stay vigilant.

How can I find the end to this chaos? she thought.

She looked back down at the letter in her hand then up at the mirror. What would you say, Mother? she asked herself.

The answer came to her in a flash.

"You mustn't only look with your eyes. You will not see the truth. You must learn to look with your heart as well."

Sugar smiled at her reflection. "Hello, Mother," she said. "I've been looking for you for a long time."

CHAPTER 21

*S*ugar found Quint in his study working as he did routinely every evening after supper. A warm glow flowed through her. She had worried many times since the tragedy of Jordan's death that she would never see this sight again. She thanked the powers that be once more for all the wonderful people who had helped make this happy moment happen.

She sat in the chair in front of his desk and waited for him to look up. His shoulder seemed to pain him less each day, she thought.

He finally set down his pen and lifted his gaze.

"Hello, Sweetie. What's on your mind?"

She sat back in the comfy chair and relaxed her head on the soft leather.

"I've been thinking," she said.

"Uh-oh," he gave a nervous chuckle.

She laughed.

"I'm serious," she said. "I'm not comfortable with the way Jordan's murder investigation has turned out."

Quint's expression turned serious.

"I know what you are talking about. I'm not feeling great about it either."

"We are acting like, 'Well, I'm okay. Who cares about anyone else?'" Sugar looked at her father for conformation.

"But that's not how we feel," he finished her thought.

"Right," she said.

He leaned forward on his elbows.

"I've been thinking. Instead of going through an expensive and lengthy trial fighting the Averills, I want to try negotiation first. I thought I could have Robert make a solid offer of restitution to them for all that has happened and include a generous offer for their ranch. The money would give them the opportunity to start over or totally change their way of life," he said. "They could wind up with enough to live comfortably for the rest of their lives. Money doesn't replace a son, but we can't do anything about that. And the money we would save by not going through a prolonged court process will cover what monies we would pay them. We could expand operations on the acquired land and even build you a house for your new husband and children."

Sugar's eyes narrowed. "Now, Daddy. Don't even start that kind of talk."

"I'm only brainstorming." He shrugged his shoulders.

"But seriously, I know what you mean. I have some ideas to the same purpose myself. Not marriage and babies, but about constructing an ending to this terrible episode of our lives. I think we can accomplish that and feel as if we had at least accepted responsibility for our share of the situation."

Quint looked at his beautiful daughter with loving pride.

"Done deal." He reached over the desk and put out his hand.

Sugar covered it with her tightest grip and shook.

"Good girl." He said shaking his hand as if she had broken it.

They laughed.

"There's another thing I need to discuss with you and you're not going to like it, but I have some important discoveries to share with you."

"Sure thing, but let's take a break and get some refreshments."

"Good idea," she said and headed for the kitchen.

They sat at the kitchen table each with a bowl of corn-bread and buttermilk and a glass of rye whiskey to wash it down.

Sugar took her mother's letter out from where she tucked it under her waistband and set it on the table in front of her father.

"Have you ever seen this?" she said.

Quint looked at the yellowed envelope with Sugar's name on the front in large letters. He did not pick it up.

"It's been a long time ago but, yes, I have seen this envelope."

"Do you know who wrote it?"

"Yes." He said.

"Have you read it?"

"It's not addressed to me," he said.

"It's addressed to me. I give you permission to read it." Sugar said.

"I don't need to read it. I know what it says."

"Read it," Sugar said again. "Please."

Quint picked up the envelope and took out the letter.

"I really don't want to read it."

Sugar insisted.

"Read it," she said.

He opened the envelope and began reading to himself. He started out fast, but the further he read, the slower his pace until he sat staring at the words all at once.

"How did you get this?" he asked. "Did Rachel give it to you?"

"No. I found it in the upstairs storage room along with a wedding trousseau and gown." And I don't know what else but I'm going to find out, she added to herself.

"What do you think of the letter? Is it true? Is this really from my mother?"

Quint picked up his glass and downed the remaining whisky in one gulp.

"Yes, I believe it is," he said.

"Why didn't't you give it to me on my eighteenth birthday?"

"Honestly, I never read the letter. Rachel brought it to me one day thirteen years ago and if I recall correctly, I told her to burn it."

Sugar's eyes narrowed and she fought the urge to scream at him.

"Why would you do that?" she said beginning to shake with suppressed anger.

"I thought she was writing to ask you to come to her. I was afraid you would run away from me like she did. I was afraid." His voice broke and tears filled his eyes. "I thought she had run away with another man. I didn't't know until now that she had been kidnapped." He began to cry.

Sugar stood and held her arms out to him. He stood slowly then hugged her to him like she was a young girl again needing her daddy's comfort.

"I was so furious at her for abandoning you, I reacted in anger and swore to protect you from her forever. She had hurt you enough. I had no idea where she would take you and what would become of you. I determined to never let that happen. At the time, I didn't't consider a grown up you. In trying to protect you and myself from any further pain, I guess I made a terrible mistake. Please forgive me!"

Quint cried so hard Sugar feared the force of the sobs would tear his gunshot wound and cause an apoplexy. She led him to his bedroom and helped him lay down. Rachel peeked around the opened door.

"You need any help?" she said her eyes wide with concern.

Sugar nodded, grateful for the offer.

Rachel left and returned with a mug of warm bourbon and lemon to sooth Quint's nerves.

"Let's prop him on these pillows. I'll hold him. You tuck in the pillows. Be careful of his shoulder."

They took their time to situate him comfortably then helped him slowly sip the sweet toddy until he had consumed it all. By then they had all calmed down. Sugar and Rachel joined him in a hot toddy, and they all sat talking quietly exchanging stories about Nicolette's kind and loving nature late into the night.

Sugar awoke curled up in the comfy overstuffed armchair in Quint's bedroom. She had planned to bring him breakfast in bed this morning but, of course, he had already dressed and gone out to inspect his ranch to make sure everything ran as smoothly as when he left three weeks ago.

After the initial emotional shock of the discussion, she thought, their talk had gone well. She felt as if a time had lapsed where between her father's responsibilities to developing the ranch and her need to get educated, and socialize with her growing up friends and activities, she and Quint had sort of lost track of each other for a while. Now that she has grown into almost adulthood, their life paths have converged again. As much fun as it was, she's not baby Sugar anymore. He's mature, successful Daddy, and she is prepared to jump into the water and see if she can swim Sugar. Like all families, they needed to hang on to the good memories and transition that loving relationship successfully into the next phase of their journey. She felt excited to see what that would be.

Sugar had just finished dressing for work when Rachel knocked on her door.

"Yes, come in," she called.

Rachel opened the door and stuck her head in.

"Good morning," she sang. "There's someone here to see you."

"Who is it," Sugar sang back in kind.

"Jim Parker," she said and closed the door.

"Parker?" she said, surprised. "What does he want," she mumbled. She picked up her hat and gun belt and walked out to see.

In the kitchen, she stopped and put her hands on her shapely hips.

"Hi, Parker. What can I do for you?" she said through gritted teeth.

Parker lounged in a chair at the table where he sat sipping a cup of coffee and talking to Rachel.

"Hello, Sugar. I was just headed back to Dallas for a new assignment, but I didn't't want to leave without making sure you were okay."

Sugar gave Rachel an I can't believe this look.

Rachel left the room to keep from laughing out loud.

"Well, goodbye Parker. Thank you for coming to help us. I'm so happy it turned out the way it did. Have a safe trip home." She shook his hand then let it drop. She tried to hide the rancor in her voice.

"Can't you come outside and talk to me for a few minutes? For the good times, for all we meant to each other?"

Sugar walked outside and stopped to stand by his horse.

Parker took her hand in his and started rubbing her arm with his other hand. "I wanted to make sure you hadn't changed your mind about coming with me."

"I haven't," she said and looked at him with a reassuring smile.

"I'm sorry I said mean things to you the last time we were together."

"We both said mean things," she said. "Don't worry about it. I'm a big girl."

"Are you sure you won't go with me?"

"If you are really worried about me, forget it. I'm where I want to be. My future is here. I have plans. Some big plans and I need to be here to get them started and keep them growing. My life is finally coming together, and I am very excited about it."

Parker looked at the ground. His heart ached as her words pummeled it, but he looked at her and smiled.

"That's wonderful to hear," he said. "I thought we had something special that day at the cove." His deep blue eyes bore into hers. But she just couldn't rise to the occasion.

"Honestly, you are one of the top three handsomest men I have ever seen. The afternoon in the cove was lovely, but you can't build a life on one kiss. Ginger told me about the two girls keeping you company when I wasn't around. Your heart isn't breaking so don't act like it is."

She continued.

"You are going to be a famous law man maybe even a lawyer someday. I hope I meet up with you and your future wife and children. She's going to adore you and you are going to adore her. You are a good man, Jim Parker, you just aren't my man. You'll see what I mean one day. You better get going. You're going to miss the best part of the travel day."

Parker felt like his heart was breaking. He had been wondering what that felt like. He had seen it happen in many women's eyes. It wasn't very nice. He almost felt guilty.

"So long, Parker." Sugar lifted his horse's reigns and handed them to him.

He let his gaze run over every inch of her then got on his horse.

"So long, Sugar," he said and rode away. Sugar turned and went back inside, not waiting to watch him go.

CHAPTER 22

Sugar logged the final dress from Nicolette's secret closet into her book and gently pressed it into the large footlocker to be stored away. When she asked Quint if she could finally relegate her mother's old possessions to storage, he told her some of the jewelry cost a good sum of money and she should keep it to wear then pass it down to her daughters, when she had them. Sugar batted her thick eyelashes at him and shook her head.

"Why do you keep talking about my children that I don't have?" she teased him.

"Because I want to make it clear that I want grandchildren. I want at least five, so you better get busy, Young Lady."

Sugar laughed.

"You're not that old," she said, "why don't you get married and have five of your own. I'll be big sister."

"Oh, Lordy!" he cried. "Never again!"

Sugar laughed until she got the hiccups

Cleared out, the room didn't't look so small.

This could be a nice office space for me, she thought imagining a Queen Anne desk and velvet covered high backed chair in a soft rose color. I'll go by Colliers and see if they have any catalogues to look at, she thought.

The day turned out so pleasantly she hadn't even noticed how quickly the time had passed. She had forgotten how smoothly life flowed when not encumbered with a crisis every day. Tonight, being Saturday night, everyone would want to go to town for some fun. She usually looked forward to playing cards, dancing, seeing all her friends, but tonight she wanted to relax, take a warm bath and maybe find a good book to read. She could also use Dad's study to work on an outline of some of the things she wanted to accomplish in the coming weeks.

In her room she laid out the bathing items, drug in the bathing tub and started heating water in the kitchen. Rachel stopped in to say bye, she wouldn't be late. Dad made no promises about time but did say good night. She heard some whooping as the ranch hands headed out. Then silence. All alone. Luxury.

The warm water felt so good when she finally stepped into the tub. She had sprinkled in some lemon bath salts and the room filled with a lovely citrus smell. She soaked her hair and scrubbed it clean then stood and lathered all over. She felt wonderful when she stepped out and toweled off. She applied cream and laid down to let it soak in.

Sugar opened her eyes and sat up. The scraping noise she had been hearing some nights had started again. But tonight, it sounded different. She heard another scrape then a tapping on the glass. There was a pattern to it, sort of a dance pattern.

Scrape, tap-tap, scrape tap-tap, scrape, tap-tap.

She had decided the noise was a possum, or some kind of animal, looking for a place to whelp some pups. But she hadn't found any evidence of a nesting animal.

Then the tattoo changed.

Tap-tap-scrape, Ta-tap-scrape, Tap-tap-scrape.

If someone wanted her, they would just have to go to the door and knock, unless this person wanted to scare her, she thought. She began to listen closer. Maybe there was a man outside the window the other night when the storm came blowing in. She did think she saw the flash of an outline of a man's shoulders and head that night. In an effort to look unaffected, Sugar walked calmly to the door and into the parlor. The heavy drapery blocked visibility from outside. The house grew silent again. She sat still and listened. Then she heard the back door open.

She jumped up immediately and ran to the front door. Trying not to make a sound, she opened the door and ran out leaving it cracked so as not to draw attention and ran as fast as she could to the bunkhouse. She opened the door and shut it quickly only to find no one there. She walked to the back door and slipped out.

She needed some place to hide, she thought, trying to keep her wits about her. She settled on the barn. Not knowing how much time she had before the creature found her, she ran as fast as she could to the side door.

Moonlight beamed through the cracks in the roof giving her enough light to see the ladder to the hayloft. If she could get up and pull the ladder after her, she might have a chance.

She stepped up on the loft floor just in time to hear the big door groan open. Not enough time for the ladder, she thought. She squatted down in a shadow at the top step and waited silently for footsteps.

She watched a man dressed all in black wearing a black face covering pull a medium sized sickle from its hook on the barn wall and walk directly over to the ladder and start climbing toward her. As he climbed, she could hear him babbling.

It sounded like he said, "I love you. You are mine. I killed Jordan for you. I almost killed Quint for you. If I can't have you no one can. You are mine now."

She tried to control her breathing as best she could. But she felt sure he heard her panting. She could hear him talking. As soon as he stepped onto the loft floor, Sugar took a deep breath and started screaming. In one swift movement she sprang up and forward with her arms extended above their heads then brought them down raking her fingernails as hard as she could along his face. He started tilting back so she put her foot square in his abdominal area and pushed as hard as she could. He fell backwards down the ladder. She flew backwards onto her backside. She started for the ladder, but not hearing any noises, she froze to listen a minute.

She heard only silence. Carefully she peeked over the opening to the floor below. A man in a black shirt and pants and a black face cover lay completely still. His legs looked tangled in odd angles and a curved sickle stuck in his neck.

She thought she saw blood pooling under his head. In a desperate attempt to not panic but get away fast, she jumped to the floor, scrambled to her feet and ran out of the barn as fast as she could, never looking back. She secured all the doors in the house and sat down and waited for someone to come home.

While waiting, she kept repeating in her mind, you can hide from the thing that scares you, but you can't hide from the fear.

The fear, she kept thinking. The fear of being alone in the world a helpless little girl without a mother. But she was old enough to be a mother, she thought. She didn't have to hang on to childish fear anymore. She had the strength now to let those fears go for good.

She stood and began cleaning her bathing equipment from the room. About an hour later, Sugar thought she heard a horse ride in. Someone knocked on the door. She walked into the kitchen and opened the door.

"Hi!" Cody said wiping his boots before stepping in the kitchen. "I was looking for you at the Cattleman. Then I saw your dad and he told me you were staying in tonight. Are you okay?"

Sugar's eyes lit up as soon as he saw his face.

"Come on in," she said pulling him into the parlor.

"Actually, I had some trouble tonight."

"What happened? Are you hurt?" he rubbed her arms and took a closer look at her face.

"No. I'm fine, I think, but I need to check on something in the barn. Would you please help me?"

"Sure," he said.

"I'm going to put on some clothes. Wait right here."

Sugar dressed in jeans, a button shirt and pulled on her boots then returned to the kitchen where Cody waited.

"Let's sit a minute so I can explain what happened."

Sugar took a breath and let it out slowly.

"Evidently, I have been having a visitor looking in my window at night."

"And you didn't tell me about it?"

Sugar stared at him for a minute.

"Was I supposed to?"

"Go on," he said not wanting to answer that question right now.

"I only realized it tonight. I heard sounds on the side of the house and tapping at the window, but I didn't't suspect a person standing out there. Between the dark outside and the glare on the window, I really couldn't't see. Then during the last storm, I walked over to the window just as a lightning bolt flared and I saw the black outline of a man's head and shoulders right outside the window. I watched the sky flash again, and he was gone. I wasn't sure if I had imagined him or he really stood there. I have been waiting to say anything until I heard the sounds again to be sure."

I heard them tonight and when I suspected it could be a prowler, I very calmly put on my robe and moved to the parlor where drapes close off the windows at night. I waited for the sounds outside, but they had stopped. A few minutes later, the back door opened..."

"The back door opened? That's enough. Take me to this man. Now!"

Sugar led Cody to the barn. The large door had swung open and Cody could see the black figure laying on the ground.

"You stay here," Cody said and walked into the barn.

Cody placed his hand on the man's chest, looked up at

her and shook his head. He stood and walked back out to join her.

"He's dead."

Sugar looked in at the body lying dead in her barn.

"I'm sorry, but it was me or him."

Cody looked at the helpless regret in her eyes.

"I understand how you feel," Cody said.

She pressed against him looking for some comfort.

He pulled her gently into his arms and hugged her tight.

Sugar exhaled a sigh of relief.

"Do you know who it was?" Cody asked her.

"I heard him talking to himself as he climbed up the ladder, but I didn't't recognize the voice."

"What did he say?"

"He said something like, "I love you. If I can't have you, no one else can. I killed Jordan, and I shot Quint. I love you. You're mine.""

"He said that? This could be Jordan's killer."

Sugar shivered.

"Go on in," he told her. "I'll close up here and be there in a minute."

"Okay." She hurried into the house.

Cody secured the barn and followed Sugar into the house.

"I think we need to leave things as they stand until we can have Grady come out and witness the scene and unmasking of the suspect."

"I agree." Sugar said.

Cody led her into the parlor. He sat on the sofa and pulled her down beside him. She cuddled up against him and tucked herself under his arm. She lay her head to rest on his shoulder. They wrapped themselves around each other and waited.

Rachel came in first. She belonged to a poker club that met the third Saturday of each month. They played for wooden nickels which they returned at the end of the evening. But they kept track of the totals and who ever had won the most wooden money received a trophy and a ranking title for the next year. Rachel enjoyed the people and the play.

Sugar saw no reason to involve Rachel in her problem tonight. They listened to Rachels evening highlights then bid her good night.

Quint finally came home around one a.m. He had gone to the Cattleman for a few hours then over to the social club to visit Ginger. Sugar explained her problem and Cody walked with him to the barn. Like Sugar and Cody, Quint had no idea what to make of this man, but he figured they better get someone official to witness the scene and let them construct an explanation to suit their requirements. With all of their problems lately, that sounded like the safest way to go.

By now, the time had waned to three a.m. and no one could find Grady. Quint decided to wait until nine a.m. when Judge Goins opened his office.

Quint said his good nights and went on to bed.

Cody stood and stretched.

"Are you going to be okay?" he said.

Sugar smiled a sleepy smile.

"Yes. Thank you for helping me again."

"My pleasure," he said. "Let me know if I can do anything else."

Sugar's heavy eyelids gave her a sultry look.

"You're such a nice man." She said softly.

Cody felt as if he had been bewitched. She had captured his heart and mind and he had no self-control left when with her. He took her hand and helped her to her feet. They walked to the kitchen and Cody led her out on the back porch. He took her into his strong embrace and kissed her with all the passion of a man desperately in love. He let her body go but kept her gaze as he looked into her eyes while walking away. She looked back enjoying the warm feeling he had aroused in her. They watched each other until he turned and walked into the bunkhouse.

"Wow," she whispered and walked slowly to her room carrying the image of his handsome face in her heart's memory.

Quint arose early and rode to town. Judge Goins arrived early to his office and invited Quint on in. Quint told him what had happened last night and that he had decided to come to him because no one could find Grady.

The judge said he would send two court investigators back with him. He thanked Quint for his wise decision to let the officials handle this.

While waiting for the investigators, Quint thought about the man in black lying dead on the floor of his old barn. If he is Jordan's killer, what was he doing following Sugar around? For how long? I wonder if she knew him. Sounds like he was crazy. This whole episode has been crazy, he thought.

The two investigators walked up.

"Mr. Wiley?" One of the men said.

"Yes, Sir, that's me," Quint said. "Just call me Quint."

The men smiled.

"I'm Grant Moliere and this is Buddy Cates. We go by Moliere and Cates."

"Glad to meet you. Thank you for helping me today. It's a messy scene."

"Let's go take a look at it," Moliere said.

They all three headed out to the Double Bar W.

Sugar met them there, but they asked her not to come in the barn until they had identified the body.

They got right to work. Each man took out a small notepad and began taking notes. Cates climbed to the hay loft to look around. Quint watched Moliere walk the barn floor intently looking for anything suspicious or contrary to the story they had been told. They deduced that Sugar ran out of the house with bare feet as she had said. Cates deduced the foot marks in the hay loft floor were consistent with Sugar's explanation of how the assailant wound up on the barn floor.

They turned their talents to the body lying in the tangled, grotesque position Sugar had left him. Moliere pulled at the tight material that covered the dead man's face and stood. The three men stared down at the bloody, twisted face of Sheriff Grady Speal, his throat slashed from front to back by the sickle he still held in his hand. All three men stared in shock at the man they had known as a good man stared back up at them with that eerie, maniacal expression on his face.

"My God," Quint said and walked out immediately to tell Sugar.

"Grady? I don't believe it," she said. "I want to see him."

"You don't want you to see him. It's too disturbing."

"If I don't see him now," she said, "I'll have nightmares of him coming for me for the rest of my life. I want to stop all this macabre foolishness. I want my life back. I want to know he can't hurt me or anyone else. I don't want to be afraid anymore."

Quint wanted to forbid her going and to send her to her room where he could lock her up and keep her safe forever from a sometimes mean and scary world. But he looked at his baby girl standing there determined to face her fear like a grown woman so she can move forward in life.

Maybe today is the day to let that happen, he thought.

"Come on, Sweetheart," he said. "Let's go kill the Boogey Man."

CHAPTER 23

S ugar awoke early and washed her face and brushed her teeth at the wash table. She had a busy day ahead, she thought excitement thrumming through her giving her extra energy for executing her plans.

Rachel had a yummy egg and sausage breakfast with a nice hot cup of coffee waiting for her. She took her time eating it.

"Where are you going today all dolled up?" Rachel said.

"I am going to start building a legacy," she said finishing her breakfast.

"Delicious eggs, thank you, Rachel," she said and walked out to saddle Magic. "We are going out today," she told the stallion and he started prancing excitedly, she thought, imitating her. She had worn her new yellow visiting dress with the draped hipline, cascading ribbon bustle and a flattering squared neckline. She felt like a ray of sunshine riding along spreading happiness to her friends and neighbors who lived in her beautiful town of Granbury. She stopped Magic in front of the bank and wound his reigns around the top of the hitching post.

Inside, the tellers and executives seemed pleased to see her. She had to hug and shake hands with each person there.

She hadn't visited her father's bank in quite a while, she thought, and she felt a little guilty about it, but her responsibilities at the ranch claimed most of her time. This morning she had scheduled an appointment with Mr. Danby, the President, to help her create what will become some of her lifetime projects.

Mr. Danby walked out of his office to greet her.

"Miss Sugar, so nice to see you," he said shaking her hand.

"Hello, Mr. Danby."

"Come in," he indicated his office, "let's see what you have here for me."

Sugar smiled and walked into the office and sat in the chair in front of his desk.

"Let's sit here at the conference table so we can work together," he said.

"Good idea," she agreed and changed to the chair he held for her.

She waited for him to sit down.

"I have made an outline explaining what I want to set up and how I want it to work. Of course, I have no training in banking so I thought I could have you advise me on what is the correct way to proceed."

He examined the outline.

"Very thorough," he said. "Are you sure you don't want

to leave the ranch to Quint and come to work here at the bank?"

They laughed.

"You have built a beautiful bank here, Mr. Danby. My father and I are very proud of what you have done," she said.

"Thank you," he nodded his head and shook her hand. "We all work to keep this the nicest bank this side of Fort Worth."

"You all are certainly doing a stellar job."

He smiled.

"Let's take a look at this," he said putting on his glasses.

Mr. Danby read the outline and asked her some questions. He had some excellent financial suggestions that made her ideas into profitable investments to allow the accounts to self-perpetuate over the years. Sugar would serve as curator of the accounts giving her flexibility and control.

One account they set up was the Wylie Fund for Civic Development which would provide funds to start initiatives to build new hospitals, schools, libraries, parks for neighbors to meet in and children to play in, projects to make the town a better place to live. Another was the Wylie Philanthropic Fund to extend loans to those who have personal needs such as crop failure, sudden illness, mortgage payment, disaster fund, resources to help the neighbors of Granbury with a safety net when trouble strikes.

When they finished, both Sugar and Mr. Danby felt very hopeful for the two endeavors and planned to work together to keep them strong and productive, a good legacy for the Wylie family to leave to the town.

"Oh, I almost forgot, the other accounts are ready to go, right?" Sugar asked.

"Yes, all set."

"Thank you for everything, Mr. Danby." She gave him a hug and left.

One more errand, she thought. The rental house turned out to be more of a rented room. The neighborhood could have been nicer, Sugar thought as she stepped up to the weathered door and knocked. Maddie Burrell, Jordan's mistress opened the door holding a newly born baby wrapped in a tattered blanket.

She looked at Sugar and frowned.

"What do you want?" she said.

"Hi Maddie. Is this Jordan, Junior?" Sugar asked.

Maddie nodded.

"May I come in and talk to you for a minute?"

"Why?" Maddie said.

"I have something to talk to you about. Please? It's important."

Maddie left the door open and walked into the front room. She sat in the only chair and looked up at Sugar.

Sugar looked around.

"How are you two doing?" she said

"How do we look?"

"Sad," she said. "I have something that might help."

"Money?"

"Yes."

"I don't need your money."

"Maybe not, but he does." Sugar pointed at the baby.

Maddie looked up at her.

"Why do you care?"

"Who says I care?" Sugar said. "Look. Just hear me out.

If you don't like my offer, don't take it. You know I didn't't kill Jordan. I had nothing to do with it. Grady Speal did it. Haven't you heard the gossip?"

"Yes."

"And I liked you. I was happy for you. I hoped you would take Jordan away."

"His parents made him stay."

"Okay. It wasn't me. Listen to me for a minute."

"All right, let me put him to bed."

Sugar waited.

Maddie came back in a better mood.

"What did you want to talk to me about?"

"Jordan and I were still married when he died. So technically I am still his widow. Your son is my stepson, technically. Since he has lost his daddy, I think Jordan would have wanted you and baby to inherit whatever he had when he died. I figured we were married four years. I thought that his son should have Jordan's share of the four-year marriage."

"I see. That makes sense," Maddie said.

"I have set up some accounts at my bank for you two. You have a household account to pay the rent, buy food, clothes, the necessities. You are going to have to take some time off to get the baby started in life. There's money for that."

"Now that you have a child to raise, you shouldn't work at the Social Club anymore. I talked to Jerry Drabber, owner of the general store on Duggan Street, to see if he had any need for a smart young lady to work for him in dry goods and lady's apparel. He said he did. And you could bring the baby to work with you."

Maddie raised her eyebrows.

"That sounds interesting."

"You need to tell him when you can start. I banked some money just for the boy in the form of a family trust. That should get him to an age where he can go out on his own. Finally, I opened an account that will pay for a good education if he wants to take that direction."

Sugar paused for a moment to catch her breath.

"I think Jordan would have approved of that. Don't you?"

Maddie looked overwhelmed.

"Yes, I do."

"Good. Here is the banker's card. Go see him as soon as possible. He will set you up. Okay?"

Maddie nodded her head.

"Okay," Sugar said. "Now Maddie, it's all up to you to make this work. Do the right thing for your son. Make good decisions. Promise me."

"I promise," she said.

Sugar smiled at her and walked to the door. She opened the door and Maddie jumped up and ran over and gave her a big hug.

"Good luck," Sugar patted her shoulder and walked out the door.

"Come and visit sometimes. Thank you" Maddie called.

Sugar smiled and waved good-bye.

CHAPTER 24

*S*ugar arrived home feeling better than she ever had in her life. She had the legacy her father had wanted so much off to a great start. She would be busier with the charities to manage, but it would be a labor of love, something her mother would have done if she had had the chance.

Quint's negotiations with the Averills were going much better than they had ever expected. The Averills had moved to Fort Worth where Constance could be close to the doctors she needed and be away from bad memories so she could work through her grief for Jordan. Robert Jakes was working closely with Arthur to come to terms on a fair settlement.

All is well at the Wylie house, she thought. On such a pretty day, a nice ride to the cove sounded relaxing. She changed into her Levi's and boots and grabbed a bottle of wine and a glass. Magic wanted to run, but Sugar kept him at a slow canter, enjoying the blooming of the summer wildflowers gathered together in patches of bright colors in shades of pink and orange and lavender and purple. Spotting a particularly beautiful grouping, she stopped and jumped off of Magic. She scooped up armfuls of the pretty blossoms and stuck them in her saddle to take home later. Magic knew where to turn into the cove. Sugar gave him his head and closed her eyes to absorb some of the warm sun.

"Hello."

She heard Cody's voice coming up behind them.

"Hello," she called back. Magic walked up under his favorite shade tree where the sweeter Johnson grass grew by the pond. Sugar slipped off of the saddle and touched the ground without disturbing the flowers.

Cody rode up on his Bay and left him in the shade grazing with Magic.

"Did you get your business done this morning?" Cody said. He laughed and brushed at the flower petals that had stuck in her silky black hair. "What is that?" he pointed at the bottle of wine.

"I just thought I'd take a nice, slow ride here and relax, have a glass of wine and watch the breeze flutter across the water."

"That does sound nice," he said sitting beside her.

He took the wine bottle, opened it and filled her glass. He took a sip and handed it to her.

She took a sip and set it down.

Cody laid down. Sugar laid down against him and rested her head on his chest. They lay in silence enjoying the humming of the dragon flies buzzing over to dip into the water and fly off to the next pond and the rhythm of each other's heart beating in sync with the day. Sugar watched the clouds changing shapes in the sky. Cody felt the softness of Sugar pressed against his side and thought how nice it would feel to run his hands all over that softness beside him. Suddenly, he sat up and rested his hands at his sides.

Sugar sat up, too.

"What's wrong?"

"Nothing," he said.

She rubbed his back.

"What are you thinking?"

He looked into her breathtakingly blue eyes, pulled her against him and kissed her until she thought she would faint.

"I can't do this," he said letting her go and running his hands through his dark blonde hair. "I want you so much. The more I'm around you, the harder it is to keep my hands off you."

"You don't like putting your hands on me?"

"I love putting my hands on you. I love being with you. I just can't have you."

"Why not?"

"Because I'm nothing but a ranch hand. I have nothing to offer you."

"Well, that's bad news," she said. "Because I was just thinking how nice it would be to marry you."

"Your father would never approve."

"Is that important? Because I've already married the man of my father's dreams. That didn't't work out so well. I thought I'd pick the man of my dreams this time. And I'm sorry but that's you."

Cody looked at her pretty face, her silver-blue eyes,

her soft luscious lips. Was she proposing to him? he thought.

He started to laugh. "Why am I arguing with you? I've been beating myself up because I couldn't't ask you to marry me because I don't have anything to offer you so you couldn't say yes. But you have plenty and you are proposing to me. So, my answer to you is yes. Yes, I will marry you."

They both fell down in the cool grass laughing.

"I don't want a big wedding," Sugar said.

Cody ran his fingers through her hair.

"Okay," he said lost in thoughts of tender nights.

"I thought we could get married Saturday."

"I don't have anything planned," he said.

"Then we could slip away and spend our wedding night here. We'll have our bed rolls for the cattle drive. Then we can have our honeymoon under the stars on the trail driving the cattle to market. What do you think?"

"I think that would be Magic." He pointed at her big black stallion.

Sugar laughed and jumped into his chest knocking him back down into the soft grass.

"You knew that all along," she said

He wrapped her in a big bear hug.

"I can finally say out loud something I've wanted to say to you for a long time," he told her, his eyes filled with happiness.

He stood, took her slender hand in his strong grasp, and started walking toward the pond. "I love you," he said and letting go of her hand, he ran and jumped into the water.

Sugar watched the man of her dreams patiently waiting for her to join him.

"I love you, too," she said and feeling the truth of those words with all her heart, she dove in after him and swam straight into his loving arms.

ABOUT THE AUTHOR

Phyllis Kerr, a native Texan, was born in San Antonio and moved with her family to Houston when she was one year old. Phyllis' mother loved to read historical romance novels, especially in her favorite Regency genre. As soon as she could read, Phyllis fell in love with romance novels, too. Over the years, she has watched so many wonderful writers develop the genre into one of the most popular today. Phyllis wrote her first novel as an homage and thank you to those past, present and future writers who carry on the tradition of Romance.

Phyllis grew up in Houston, attended Bellaire High School and made her home in the Clear Lake City area. She earned her Bachelor of Arts degree in literature from The University of Houston—Clear Lake while helping her husband build a business and raising two sons. She has worked in the family business, taught English and English as a second language and now enjoys writing, spending time with her husband of fifty years, two sons, three grandchildren and loving cat, ChaCho.

Made in the USA
Columbia, SC
07 February 2021